I0699677

GLITCHING THE MATRIX

Also by Megan Bledsoe

Glitching the Matrix: *a novel . . .*
The Metanaut: *a supernatural thriller*
Girl, Incorrupted: *a love-horror story*

THE *CORBIN KOHL IN HELL* SERIES
fun low-fantasy mysteries
Corbin Kohl Adrift in Hell
Corbin Kohl Baited in Hell
Corbin Kohl Cornered in Hell

MEGAN BLEDSOE

GLITCHING THE MATRIX

Arched Brow Books

VANCOUVER

This is a work of fiction.
Names, characters, places, and incidents either are the product of the author's imagination or are used fictitiously. Any resemblance to actual persons, living or dead, events, or locales is entirely coincidental.

GLITCHING THE MATRIX

Copyright © 2026 by Megan Bledsoe

The moral right of the author has been asserted.

Published by Arched Brow Books
Arched Brow Books is a trademark of Arched Brow Publishing

All rights reserved.
No part of this book may be reproduced or used in any manner whatsoever without the prior written permission of the copyright owner.

Designed by Megan Bledsoe

Cover design elements by alexsl (numbers) via Canva.com
and by artawkrn (female head) via Pixabay.com
Ending text image by GDJ via Pixabay.com
Cover and text typefaces by Vernon Adams (Anton), Georg Duffner (EB Garamond), Hector Gatti (Saira Stencil One), Steve Matteson (Open Sans, Tinos), and Pria Ravichandran (Palanquin) via fonts.google.com
and by Emily Conners (Bergamot Ornaments) via myfonts.com

Bledsoe, Megan, 1980–
Glitching the Matrix / by Megan Bledsoe.
First Edition. | Vancouver : Arched Brow Books, 2026.
FICTION / Thrillers / Supernatural
FICTION / Visionary & Metaphysical
FICTION / Surrealism

Summary: When a suburban soccer mom experiences a series of small unexplainable events some call glitches in the matrix, she sets out to make reality glitch on purpose; and someone—or something—takes notice.

ISBN 978-1-969265-08-2 (hardcover)
ISBN 978-1-969265-07-5 (epub)

For the curious and observant

GLITCHING THE MATRIX

Chapter 1

Still half asleep, Karen Baker turned the upward-pointing chrome shower valve handle a fraction to the right, and hot, steamy water poured from the spout. She pulled up the diverter. Water gurgled as the showerhead sputtered to life. The stream thumped against the tub, making a limp arc that barely reached the center of the basin.

Karen groped for her phone on the bathroom counter behind her and typed out a text to her husband.

> We really should fix the water pressure in the shower.

She hit send and set the phone back on the counter, not waiting for a response. He wouldn't send one.

She pulled back the double shower curtain. The front-facing layer was thick and white, with a terry cloth texture that had reminded Karen of a luxurious spa when she'd first seen it on sale in her last year of law school. She'd had dreams of remodeling her first home's bathroom to look more like a spa: white marble instead of this beige laminate counter and linoleum flooring, glass vessel sinks instead of these chipped ones with their yellowing calk, something better than the cheap-looking chrome fixtures. But that dream was almost ten years old now, and the frayed bottom of the white terry cloth was all grubby from being pulled on by two finger-painting kids.

Karen still liked how thick and luxurious it felt, though. She stepped into the hot water and pulled the curtain shut behind her, tilted her face up to the weak stream.

"Wake up, Karen."

Karen wrapped the towel around her wet hair and padded into her bedroom.

The light in the room flickered.

The only light on in the room was the upward-facing light in the ceiling fan. Paul flicked that light on when he was getting ready for work because Karen could easily sleep through it. Its light was like an oversized candle. Its three little bulbs created three overlapping circles of light on the ceiling and cast diffused light everywhere else.

But it wasn't the light in the ceiling fan that was flickering; the three overlapping light circles steadily shined.

It was only the diffused light that was flickering. Like a reverse strobe. Dimmer, instead of brighter.

Karen rubbed her eyes, but when she opened them again, the room was still flickering. Like a slowed-down movie reel. It was barely perceptible and yet definitely happening.

But it was probably just some flickering light from one of the backyard neighbors.

One glance at the bedroom window mostly confirmed it.

The curtain was cracked open. There was pitch-black glass between the tawny panels.

She looked back at her room, and the flickering was gone.

Yeah. The curtain was open. It was probably just someone else's dying light.

The house was silent. Paul had offered to take the kids in early this morning so that she could relax and focus and prepare. So kind of him. She would pick Lila and Kyle up from school as usual, but until then, the day was hers.

She got dressed in the outfit she'd selected the night before, a dark gray suit that she hoped said she was serious about working again but not so serious as to be a dull colleague and office mate.

Now that her youngest was finally in school, she could go back to work. She'd thought she'd be able to work right away after Lila was born. Not necessarily because she wanted to, but because needs must. She'd had dreams of renovated bathrooms and professionally landscaped lawns. But daycare cost almost as much as she'd been making as a first-year associate at a small firm before going on maternity leave. Add in all the time and gas used up in dropping the kids off and picking them up again—not to mention the mental bandwidth of having to coordinate it all—and it just didn't make any sense for her to not stay home.

"It's just until Lila's in school," Paul had said.

"Yeah, but by then, there will just be more, younger, hungrier, less-strapped graduates to choose from."

"You can't think about it like that."

Except she could, and she did. Until Kyle came along, and he and Lila together had her giggling and playing on the floor and giving up the idea of ever being a successful anything-but-a-mom at all. Karen was mostly okay with the decision. A good mom was a good thing to be.

But that decision apparently wasn't hers to make, either.

She had cast her net wide, applying for associate jobs and in-house staff counsel, but also for non-attorney jobs. Positions with the school or the county or just the mom-and-pop shop down the street. Because needs must. Extracurricular activities and keeping up with technology were expensive. If Paul had gotten a big fancy-schmancy law firm job, not only would he probably have made enough money that she wouldn't have had to work at all, but he could've gotten her hired, too, when she was ready.

But no. Paul worked at the county prosecutor's office.

It was a good fit, if she was being honest. He wasn't the stuffed-shirt type. He liked the building's rundown facade and salt-of-the-earth people. He liked being tough but fair and compassionate. He liked the job. And he was good at it. She was proud of him.

Now if only she could find something to do that would allow her to feel proud of herself.

Karen climbed into the driver's seat of her ten-year-old SUV and shut herself inside. She sighed and leaned her head against the steering wheel, thankful that she'd parked in a darker part of the law firm's parking garage.

She'd done the best she could. And it wasn't truly over until they called—or not—and told her she didn't get the job. Until then, she'd done the best she could. And having done the best she could, she could still hold on to hope.

She turned on the car and reversed out of the parking spot.

The law firm was just the kind of thing Karen aspired to. The office took up the top five floors in a beautiful glass building that claimed an entire city block downtown. It even had its own free parking. Its own gym, too. The five associates she'd met with were all trim and smiling, with firm handshakes. Hers had gone embarrassingly limp gripping each one.

You did the best you could.

And she had. She'd prepared for the inevitable question about what she'd been doing the past eight years since leaving her first post-law-school job after only eleven months.

"I took a planned pause to focus on my daughter and son, but now that they're both in school, I'm eager to get back to work."

Her interviewers nodded, but she felt their disbelief, saw it in their raised eyebrows. *Oh, you're asking us to believe* that *fiction?*

Because of course it was a fiction. A planned pause? Nothing about kids could be planned. And now she had two to plan around.

The rest of the interview had felt the same. The questions perfunctory. Her answers merely adequate. She felt no spark. No connection with the people on the other side of the table.

They'd shown her around the office anyway. They'd introduced her to partners, shown off building's perks, added insult to injury.

She'd thanked them profusely. For their time. For their consideration. She didn't just shake their hands, but gripped them tightly with both of hers, like maybe she could infuse in them the desire to hire her.

Ah well. Better luck next time and all that. She headed into midtown to have lunch with the girls.

It was mid-October, and the autumn leaves were in full color. Summer was still holding on in terms of keeping the sky blue and the rain at bay, but it was starting to get cold. Not so cold that she and Paul had turned on the heat yet, but cold enough that they bundled everyone up in hoodies and socks around the house.

She pulled into the Panera's parking lot, taking a spot next to a new silver Rivian. A new, all-black Escalade was parked next to it. Skyler and Hannah were already here.

Karen had been hoping to go home before lunch so that she could change out of her suit, but the office tour had left her too little time. She thought about leaving her suit jacket in the car. But going inside in just her button-up would draw its own questions, which would eventually clue the girls into her interview. She leaned into the backseat and rifled through her workout bag, even though she knew there was nothing useful in there. She should've packed a cardigan or something.

Too late now.

She shut the door and locked the car with her key fob. It honked back at her.

She passed Cecily's Range Rover on her way inside the restaurant. A guy in his twenties held the door open for her.

The lobby smelled of fresh-baked bread and coffee. She heard the *pssshhh*-ing sound of a barista frothing milk. A clerk stocking the display case dropped a croissant.

The girls were all standing back from the counter, staring up at the menu, even though they ordered the same thing every week.

They turned around at the sound of the door opening.

"There you are," Cecily said. Then she blinked at Karen. "Why are you wearing a suit?"

Cecily was wearing an oversized ruched shirt under a cropped denim jacket, paired with black leggings and gray booties, and she had a tiny red purse pulled up over one shoulder. Her latest delivery from an online personal styling service, no doubt. Diamonds and other jewelry glittered on her hands.

Hannah and Skyler looked similar, although with smaller bits of sparkle. Hannah's leggings looked more sporty, like she was ready to go to the gym after this, which she probably was, and Skyler's purse was a giant carpet-textured Mary Poppins-style thing that held everything and weighed a ton.

Before Karen could answer, Cecily leaned toward her and said in an accusatory tone, "Did you have an interview?"

"Yup," Karen said. Might as well just get it over with. "With Martin, Tyler, and Gray."

"You're kidding?" Cecily said, sounding both impressed and disbelieving.

Cecily's husband worked at the second largest firm in town and hadn't even gotten an interview at Martin Tyler. But rather than letting that fact stroke her ego, Karen saw it as just another reason to doubt they would hire her.

"How'd it go? You look good," Cecily said.

"Very professional," Skyler added with a smile.

"Thanks." Karen smiled back, then shrugged. "It went. Let's order. I'm starved."

Karen ordered a poppy-seed bagel. It was the cheapest thing on the menu. The girls ordered salads and lattes. They sat at their usual table, the middle one next to the window, so that they could see and be seen and keep an eye on Hannah and Skyler's new cars.

Karen listened politely while Hannah and Skyler debated the merits and disappointments of their chosen new vehicles, and Cecily decreed that they should've spent a little more money and gotten a lot more car.

Adding celebrities to the topic of conversation transitioned them from talking about which celebrities supposedly drove which cars to which celebrities were caught up in the latest trend that had recently taken over their kids' schools. Cecily and Hannah's daughters were obsessed with some ugly eight-inch doll that reminded Karen of the gotta-have-it craze of Russ trolls that had hijacked her and her friend's imaginations back when she was in early elementary school. Karen had used her allowance to buy as many trolls as she could, from the baby troll in diapers to the granny troll with a cane—Russ trolls only, please; no knock-offs. Then there'd been the Beanie Babies craze that had taken over some time in junior high or high school. She'd fallen hard for the tiny Beanie Babies they'd offered in McDonald's Happy Meals. Karen had collected them all. Too bad she'd kept them all in the back window of her first car, or they might've been worth something now. And let's not forget the Tickle Me Elmos that had later become all the rage. That craze had unwittingly added the genius element of scarcity, which really fired up the mania.

This new craze had all that and something more: an element of disappointment framed as mystery, luck, and surprise. Each doll came in a solid box with no sheer window, so shoppers couldn't see and select the doll they wanted. Meanwhile, the company made sure to let consumers know that certain of the dolls were rare.

Cecily said, "I've ordered Corrine at least a dozen of those damn dolls, and she still hasn't gotten the one she wants."

"Heather has it," Hannah said.

"Yes, I know Heather has it," Cecily said. "Corrine knows she has it. Everyone knows she has it. Thank you for that."

Hannah shrugged smugly.

Karen thanked God every day that Lila was so dedicated to ballet that she hadn't gotten sucked into any of this fanfare yet. Yeah, Karen had to buy dance classes and tights and leotards and toe shoes and cotton padding and costumes and recital tickets. But at least her daughter was learning something and having fun and getting some exercise. At best, any iteration of the latest doll craze would stay sealed up in their boxes and get placed up on a high shelf only to get pulled down again just long enough to be shown off to visitors or put up for sale for much less than the collector was hoping they'd eventually be worth.

But talking about dolls was better than the topic the conversation veered toward next.

"She's living in a mud hut."

"No."

"Yes," Cecily insisted.

When she couldn't take anymore doll talk, Karen had excused herself to go to the ladies' room, and now, as she made her way back to the table, she could hear that the girls were obviously talking about Sophie. Sophie and her husband had recently moved their family out of their four-garage, four-bathroom house in Golden Hills to some property out in the boonies.

"You've seen her?" Karen asked as she reclaimed her seat. "How's she doing?"

"Living in a mud hut," Skyler whispered to Karen, helpfully catching her up.

"She's *homesteading,*" Cecily said, giving the word air quotes. "And yet still driving that custom eye-sore of hers." Sophie drove a Jeep Grand Wagoneer with a custom white-to-pink, color-changing chameleon paint job. She bought it for herself after landing a plum in-house counsel job right out of law school. Just the thought of that huge cotton-candy car made Karen snicker. "I saw her and Sara in it just the other day," Cecily finished.

"Lila says Sara isn't in school anymore," Karen said.

"Nope, she took them out," Cecily said. "She's *homeschooling* them now."

"Why?" Hannah asked.

But the bigger question was why hadn't Sophie told anyone beforehand? She'd just disappeared one day.

Cecily shrugged like she couldn't deal with it anymore and Sophie was in God's hands now.

But that didn't stop Cecily from talking about it. If anything, it only fueled the fury. Between tiny bites of crunchy salad, Cecily went round and round for the rest of the meal, complaining about Sophie leaving and what Sophie coulda, woulda, shoulda done differently to avoid having to move to the middle of nowhere and miss lunches like these.

Karen's bagel was long since finished, and her trusty if ten-year-old car was just outside. She stared at it longingly, dutifully nodding her agreement with everything that was said and wondering what it would be like to live on a homestead—whatever that was.

Outside, a young woman with a striking blond ponytail was walking past the far window—and she suddenly froze mid-stride.

Karen narrowed her eyes and studied her: the textbook clutched to her chest and the phone tucked into the back pocket of her jeans. She was looking off across the street. She had probably just noticed something that had so caught her attention, it had literally stopped her in her tracks.

But something about the woman still seemed odd. Karen was about to nudge Skyler and point the woman out to her when the woman started moving again. She stepped off the curb and got into her red VW Bug, her ponytail wagging from side to side.

So it was nothing, then.

Even if something about it still felt odd.

It would be days before Karen realized it wasn't just the woman who had stopped mid-stride, but her ponytail, too. It had stopped mid-swing, parallel to the ground, high on the left side of her head.

$\mathbf{B}$ack in her SUV and sitting on a towel, all sweaty from spending two hours at the gym—first on a StairMaster, then in an aerobics class, and then moseying tiredly between weight machines—Karen went to pick up her kids.

The single-story red elementary school was in a heavily treed residential neighborhood with lots of squirrels, and at pick-up time, it was a madhouse.

Between all the buses lined up along the front entrance and all the parents sitting bumper to bumper, trying to squeeze into the parking lot, there was no room to breathe, let alone park.

Karen took a side road and parked in her usual spot two blocks away. She got out, cleaned up the back seat, collecting trash and tossing toys into the back, and then she walked up to the school. She figured Lila was responsible enough, and Kyle old enough, for the two of them to find each other out front, grab hands, and then meet her at the car. But school policy (or parent-to-parent shame; she wasn't sure which) necessitated that no child leave school property without a chaperone.

So she met them at the corner: the right-front corner of the school, where a double-slat metal railing followed the street's sidewalk and then curved ninety degrees to guard part of the school's front walkway from a slight decline that dipped down to the parking lot and the bus loop that circled it. The hill was landscaped with bark dust and young leafless trees planted forty feet apart.

Karen wasn't the only parent who'd had the genius idea to meet their kids at the corner.

"Hey, Karen," one of the moms said as Karen reached the meeting spot.

"Hey, Molly."

"Will I see you at the T-ball game tonight?"

"Oh, shit."

Molly laughed. A couple of the other parents tut-tutted. Karen ignored them.

"It's my turn for snack duty, too," Karen said. "Shoot. Thanks for reminding me."

"No problem. Perfect timing," Molly added as she pointed through the school crowd.

Lila and Kyle were bounding toward them down the sidewalk.

Karen dropped into a crouch and opened her arms wide, taking both kids in at once and wrapping them up in a giant hug. Kyle hugged her back while Lila mostly stood awkwardly. She was entering that age. They smelled like glue and fresh earth and pencil shavings. She squeezed them tighter, then stood up and took Kyle's warm, soft hand, letting Lila walk by herself.

"See you at T-ball," Molly said.

"Yes," Karen said, having already forgotten again. "T-ball. Yes." She shook Kyle's hand. "You've got T-ball tonight. Right, buddy?"

"Yup."

She looked back up at Molly. "Thank you. See you later, Molly."

"See ya."

Once everyone was all buckled up and they were on the road, Karen asked them about the funnest thing they'd done in school that day. Kyle said, "Recess." It was his usual answer. But Lila told Karen about a game her class was playing.

"First we took a test. Whoever got the highest grade on the test, gets to be the bank."

"Was that you?"

"Yeah. Me and Eloise. Then the next highest grade gets to be employers. I don't know what they do. And then everyone else gets to be employees, and they all have to do a lot of worksheets."

"What do you and Eloise do?"

"Nothing."

Karen glanced at Lila in the rearview mirror. She was leaning into the center of the bench seat.

"Nothing?" Karen asked.

Lila shrugged. "We take people's money when they give it to us."

Karen stopped at a slow, red left-turn light at an intersection with no traffic.

"They teach you that in third grade, huh?"

The kitchen was cleaner than Karen had left it. She figured Paul must've forgotten his lunch in the upheaval of taking the kids with him this morning, and had come home to eat it.

Karen texted him to remind him about the T-ball game, and then she got the kids fed and focused on their homework.

"I'll be down in a minute if you need help," she said. "I'm just gonna take a quick shower."

She went upstairs and peeled off her workout clothes, then pulled back the thick white shower curtain. She turned the shower valve handle a fraction to the right and put her hand under the spout. The water was cold.

She turned on the water in the sink to get it heating up faster. But the water in the sink was already hot. She turned it back off and put her fingers under the water pouring from the tub spout again.

Still cold.

Well, that didn't make any sense. If the sink water was hot, then the shower water should also be hot.

She could make the water hotter by pointing the valve handle closer to the twelve o'clock position, but the handle was barely pointing to one o'clock as it was. Moving it closer to twelve o'clock would lighten up the already weak water pressure and then turn the water all the way off completely.

She turned the handle all the way to the right until it was pointing to five o'clock. The water roared out of the faucet and got very, very cold—and then it turned off at six o'clock.

Had it always turned off at six o'clock? Karen couldn't remember. She'd never needed to turn it that much.

Karen slowly turned the valve handle back up toward one o'clock. The water turned back on, but it didn't get any hotter. She kept turning the handle: Twelve thirty. Twelve o'clock. The water didn't turn off. It should have, but it didn't turn off.

"What the...?"

She turned the knob past twelve o'clock, toward eleven o'clock.

The pressure remained high, and the water turned hot. She could see the steam rising.

She grinned and stepped under the steamy, powerful spray.

Paul must've come home and fixed the faucet. What a guy.

Paul was home when she got out of the shower. She could hear him downstairs with the kids.

"There's spaghetti on the stove," she called down.

"I had some, thanks," he called back. "T-ball at six?"

"Yeah. I'll be ready in a second."

"No rush."

Karen dressed in jeans and a hoodie and went downstairs. Her clean feet stuck to the hardwood floors. She found the three of them sitting at the table, playing a card game.

"Hey," she said, pecking Paul on the cheek. "Thanks for fixing the faucet."

"What faucet?"

He played a card, and both kids said, "Ohhh!"

Karen went into the kitchen and dug out her yellow mixing bowl. The trilevel's main floor was open-concept; only a small, freestanding pantry and a peninsula counter separated the kitchen from the table where Paul and the kids were sitting. So it was easy to keep talking.

"The shower faucet," Karen said. "The hot-water pressure is great now."

Karen dug out her hand mixer and her recipe for brownies, and then she searched the pantry for ingredients, putting the sugar, flour, and vanilla on the counter.

Paul said, "I didn't fix the faucet."

"You didn't?"

"No."

"Didn't you come home for lunch?"

"Yeah."

Karen waited a beat, then peeked around the pantry at the kitchen table. "But you didn't fix the faucet?"

"No. You sure it's fixed?"

Karen ran a gripped fist over a hank of her wet hair and flung the collected water at Paul.

"Hey!"

"Yeah," she said with a laugh. "I'm sure it's fixed. You didn't fix it?"

"No."

"Well, it's fixed anyway."

She dug eggs and butter out of the fridge.

"What are you doing?" Paul asked.

"Making brownies. It's our turn to bring snacks."

"Yay!" Kyle said, pumping his fists in the air.

Paul said, "Have we got time? We could just pick something up on the way."

"*Oh*, no, we can't. They have to be *homemade* snacks. Trust me. If they're not, you might not get called out for it, but I'll get an earful."

"What about allergies? Won't you get an earful about allergies?"

"We're bringing oranges, too. They're already in the car."

She mixed the sugar and butter and then cracked the first egg into the bowl.

Her phone rang. She could hear it in the bedroom.

She set the eggshells on the counter, grabbed the towel off the oven handle, and wiped her hands with it as she went upstairs to answer the phone.

Her phone was on her dresser, but it stopped ringing before she could reach it. She checked the number. It wasn't anyone already programmed into her phone, and she didn't recognize the number. The caller would have had to dial twice in order to get it to ring—and it looked like they had—but they hadn't left a message. She took her phone with her downstairs, thinking maybe they were leaving a long message. But the phone remained silent.

"Who was it?" Paul asked from the kitchen table.

"Spam, I guess. They didn't leave a message."

She placed the phone on the counter and returned to her mixing bowl. She picked up the egg and brought it to the side of the bowl, preparing to crack it, but then she noticed something was off:

"Didn't I already crack this?"

"What?"

"This egg." She lifted the wooden spoon out of the bowl. The brown mixture was still gritty. Just butter and sugar. "I could have sworn I was cracking this egg when the phone rang."

"Okay," Paul said.

"No, really. I cracked the egg, dropped the egg goop into the bowl. I got it on my hands! I took the towel upstairs with me!"

She pointed at the towel hanging on the oven handle, but it wasn't there, because she'd taken it upstairs to her room.

She ran up there now, scanned the surfaces of her bedroom.

There. She'd left the towel where the phone had been. She carried it back downstairs and waved it around like proof.

Paul and the kids had gotten up from the table and were hanging around the mixing bowl. Lila was holding the recipe's eggs.

"You've got two eggs here," Paul said. "What are you going on about?"

"I cracked one of them," Karen said. "I cracked it into the bowl. I could swear to it. But there's no egg in here."

Karen showed them the bowl of brown gritty mixture.

"Maybe you stirred it in," Lila said.

"I didn't, though," Karen said. "You can tell that I didn't. See all that grit? Egg is what makes the batter smooth."

Lila nodded.

Paul had an odd look on his face.

"What are you thinking?" Karen asked.

"You really cracked the egg?" he asked.

Had she?

"I mean, yeah, I think so. Ninety-nine percent sure. I took the towel upstairs with me."

Paul said, "We can check if you cracked the egg."

"How?"

He pointed at a camera mounted above the refrigerator. She knew he'd placed cameras at the front door and over the garage, but she didn't know he'd placed them around the house.

"When did you put that there?"

"Same time as the others. It's watching the French doors"—which were on the other side of the kitchen counter, to the left side of the kitchen table—"but the camera probably picked you up, too, at the counter."

Karen glanced up at the camera and tried to follow its line of sight. It seemed promising. "Can we look?"

"Yeah." Paul dug out his phone and opened an app. The kids tugged on him until he squatted down so that they could look over his shoulder.

"Well?" Karen asked.

"It's not a very good angle," Paul said as he and the kids watched the feed all the way through.

"Let me see," Karen said.

Paul stood up and handed Karen the phone. They watched it together.

The camera had captured Karen's right side, from the back, and it showed the yellow mixing bowl on the counter, with all the ingredients set up around it.

The replay showed Karen picking up a stick of butter. The angle wasn't good enough to see her unwrap the butter and drop it into the bowl, but it showed her setting the waste wrapper on the counter. She then measured out the sugar. And then she ran the hand mixer, holding it in her right hand. Her left hand would've been scraping down the bowl, but that wasn't visible either.

She set the mixer on the counter, leaving the beaters hanging over the inside of the bowl.

Then there was a moment where she looked like she was doing nothing. And then her right hand reached over the bowl, right before she looked over her shoulder at something past the camera.

"That must've been when the phone rang," she said.

Karen couldn't see what she'd been doing with her left hand, her dominant hand. Whether she'd set down empty eggshells or a whole, intact egg before going to answer the phone, she couldn't tell.

But as she'd turned toward the camera, her right hand had grabbed the towel off of the oven handle. And she'd wiped her hands with it as she'd walked out of view.

"It looks like you probably picked up the egg but didn't crack it," Paul said.

"Except I did crack it," she said, because the video had made her more certain than ever. "Watch it again. Just the part after I finish mixing."

Paul rewound to that point.

Onscreen, Karen set down the hand mixer. Then she stood still for two or three seconds.

"Rewind it again."

Paul did.

She stood still for two or three seconds, but for the first of those seconds, her left elbow popped into view behind her.

Karen pointed at the screen. "That's me picking up the egg."

And then her right hand rose over the bowl.

She touched the screen, pausing the video.

"See that?"

"It's kinda hard to see anything."

"Come on. How do you crack an egg? Here. Crack this egg. Into the bowl."

She handed Paul one of the recipe's two eggs. He cracked it on the side of the bowl with his right hand and then brought up his left hand to pry the shell halves apart—but Karen stopped him before he could.

"See! You brought up your other hand to pull open the egg. You would only do that if you'd already cracked it."

She rewound the video a couple seconds and played it again. Her left elbow poked out, and then a second or two later she brought up her right hand.

Then she looked over her shoulder and grabbed the towel.

"I cracked that egg," she said.

"Okay," Paul said. "You cracked the egg. And?"

Karen gaped at him. "Well, isn't that weird?"

"I guess."

"You still don't believe me."

"I believe you."

Karen sighed. He didn't believe her. Or he did, but he didn't comprehend the significance.

Although… she wasn't sure she did either. She merely felt it. It felt significant. She'd cracked the egg. But then it had—what?—glued itself back together? It was unfathomable. But if she couldn't explain it to herself, then how was she expecting Paul to understand?

She glanced at the time on the microwave.

"It's too late to finish these. Do you want to stop and pick something else up for snacks or just roll with the oranges?"

Chapter 3

They rolled with the oranges. Paul drove, and Karen stared out the window, thinking about the egg, running over her movements in her mind.

Maybe she'd *thought* she had cracked it, but really, she hadn't.

But no, she recalled the egg yolk plopping into the bowl, the eggshell cracking further in her hands and getting leftover egg white on fingers. She mimed wiping her hands now, as she remembered wiping them on the towel on her way up the stairs.

She'd cracked that egg.

Tonight's T-ball game was held at Treeline Park. A paved loop separated the playing fields on the outside from the central area, which was filled with cedar and oak trees and included a fenced playground for little kids and a bigger playground for bigger kids.

Tonight's game wasn't an officially sanctioned game. Fall Ball didn't have any official games; it was just an opportunity for kids who preferred baseball to soccer to stay active into the autumn. This game was just a meet-up between two coaches who were friends and who understood that kids preferred to play rather than practice.

Paul and Karen set up camp chairs in front of the cyclone fence, beside the dugout.

When Molly arrived, she asked if she could set up her chair beside Karen's.

"Of course."

Molly set down her chair and unfolded it.

Paul, basically a big kid himself, took advantage of Karen having other company and excused himself from watching the game while Kyle was on the bench, having already had his turn at bat. Paul wandered away to go explore the trees and check on Lila, who was playing with some of the other older siblings at the big-kid park. And he'd probably check out the snacks at the nearby convenience store, too, there being no brownies and all.

"Sorry," Molly said, gesturing to Paul as he walked away.

"Oh, don't worry about him. He thanks you for the excuse to leave. He'll be back when the kids are out on the field again, but he can't sit still for more than two minutes otherwise. Thanks again, by the way, for the reminder about the day."

"No problem."

One of the kids made it to base, and Molly clapped. Karen had been thinking about the egg again, and her clap came late.

"Everything okay?" Molly asked.

Karen considered Molly—her mom jeans, her red school-emblazoned sweatshirt from several years ago, her not-trying-to-impress-anyone dark hair twirled up in a knot on her head—and figured, what the hell. Unlike the tut-tutters, Molly had laughed when Karen had cursed on the school corner. And Karen was dying for someone to understand what she'd experienced with the egg.

She turned toward Molly. "Something weird happened while I was making brownies."

"Do I want to know?"

"What do you mean? Oh, with the brownies? They didn't get made. The batter's in the—never mind. We brought oranges. Thing is, I cracked the first egg into the bowl, but then I got a phone call. So I went upstairs. But when I came back"—she paused for effect—"the egg was whole again."

"No shit?"

"Yes!" Karen said, and she grabbed Molly's hands. Molly had offered exactly the sentiment Karen had been expecting, and she couldn't be more grateful. "Thank you. I told Paul, and he was all..." Karen pulled a face and shrugged. "But he tells me he's got a camera set up to watch the back door and that it probably picked up the whole thing. So we look at it. And I shit you not, it shows me cracking the egg."

"You're kidding? Can I see?"

Karen reached for her phone and then remembered: "I don't have the app. Paul's got it on his phone. But it doesn't actually show me cracking the egg. It shows me from the side. You can't really see the egg. But I'm standing there long enough to crack the egg, and then my other hand comes up. You know, to pull the shell apart. You would only bring up that second hand if you had already cracked the egg and now had to pull it apart. Right?"

Molly made a face, like she'd made brownies a million times and was running through the motions in her head.

"Yeah," she said.

"See?" Karen sat back in her chair, satisfied that someone believed her. Another kid made it to base, and this time Karen leaned forward and clapped on cue and yelled, "Good job."

"Anything else weird happen today?"

Karen settled back in her seat and looked at Molly. "What do you mean?"

Molly shrugged. "I don't know. Anything?"

Something had immediately popped into Karen's mind. She considered it, and then said it out loud. "The water on the shower was fixed."

"How so?"

"It's the shower in the master bath. The nozzle was set up to turn on hot and then get cooler the more you turn it. But the hot water pressure sucked. It's been that way since we moved in. But I took a shower after I picked up the kids, and it was fixed. Paul said he didn't do it."

"And you believe him?"

Karen laughed. "Yeah. He didn't do it. Why do you ask?"

"How weirded out are you about the egg?"

"Pretty weirded out. It's weird, isn't it? Isn't it weird?"

"It's very weird. And you seem relieved to be taken seriously."

"Paul didn't exactly blow me off, but... yeah... he didn't get it. The egg *put itself back together*. I'm sorry, but that's just weird. That kinda thing just doesn't happen."

"Not usually, no."

"Not *usually*? What are you talking about?"

Molly said, "Are you busy tomorrow?"

Chapter 4

The next day was Thursday, and, no, Karen wasn't busy. At least, not while the kids were at school.

After dropping them off, Karen met Molly at the Starbucks on Powell. She got there first and went inside. The line was long, so she sat at a small circular table by the window to wait for the line to dwindle and to watch for Molly.

Molly pulled up right in front of her window, in a dusty old silver Camry with a red front fender.

Karen waved.

Molly beckoned her outside.

Karen grabbed her purse and excused herself through the line, then pushed her way out the door. She met Molly at the curb.

"Everything okay?" Karen asked.

"Yeah. We're not going to Starbucks."

"Oh, we're not?"

"Not unless you want something. Did you want something?"

Karen looked back at the store. There was a period of several years when her second home had been a coffee shop. She'd been looking forward to the excuse to get a pumpkin spice latte. They were in season, after all. But she shook her head no.

"Do you want to follow me or ride with me?" Molly said.

"Where are we going?"

"It's out in Bullworth."

"*Bullworth*?" Karen exclaimed. Bullworth was within the county, but there was only one road that led to the area, and it wound through the woods at thirty miles an hour, so it took forever to get there.

"That okay?" Molly asked.

Karen had thought about the egg all night. She'd had Paul send her the surveillance clip so that she could watch it on repeat on her own phone. She'd counted the seconds between her left elbow popping into view and her right hand moving over the bowl to help pull the shell apart. It had taken her 1.8 seconds. She wasn't an egg-cracking pro. She was just an average baker who hadn't been in a hurry. Others could've done it faster and with just the one hand. She'd watched them on YouTube. But their speed compared to her speed just convinced her even more that she most definitely had cracked that egg.

"You sure you didn't fix the faucet?" she'd asked Paul that morning from the bed after he got out of the shower.

"Nope. It's nice, though. Maybe the shower fairies did it. Or something in the knob slipped."

She'd thought about that, about something in the knob slipping. But why would it? And how could it have? The faucet wasn't dripping. It was just fixed.

And when she'd come out of the bathroom herself, she'd seen the flickers again, the strobe effect dimming her room rather than brightening it.

"Yeah, it's okay," she said to Molly. "Let's go to Bullworth." She looked back at her SUV. She didn't like feeling dependent, but she also didn't like to drive those tight turns through the woods, especially in her old SUV. It had a tendency to rock. "Can I go with you?"

"Of course. Get in." Molly ducked back into her car and reached across the front seat to unlock the front passenger door.

Karen aimed her key fob at her SUV. It blinked and honked back at her, confirming it was locked. She opened the Camry's front passenger door and climbed inside. Molly had the heat on, and the warm air blew the scent of a strawberry tree air freshener.

They made small talk as Molly drove through town. Aside from seeing each other at the school corner and at T-Ball games, they didn't really know each other. Molly said she was a single mom to Cole and that Cole's dad wasn't in the picture. She didn't elaborate as to why, and Karen didn't ask her to. Not that she wasn't interested. It was just that Molly seemed to be really concentrating on the road, leaning this way and that as she checked traffic, road signs, and blind spots. And when the woods came into view and they turned onto Bullworth Drive, Karen didn't want to distract her. Some of the road's curves had some pretty scary drop-offs.

They drove up the road for miles.

"How far is it?" Karen asked.

"Out at the end. Not the end-end—that's Winehauer property. The forest products company?"

"Right."

"But just before that."

Karen nodded, even though she still didn't know how much longer the drive would be. She'd never been out to the end of Bullworth Drive.

The drive was beautiful in mid-autumn. The trees lining the

road included evergreens, like pines and cedars, but also a lot of maples that were just starting to lose their leaves. The mid-autumn skies were still blue, and occasionally the mid-morning sun would break through the trees and highlight the red, orange, and yellow leaves on the maples. Just beautiful.

"Almost there," Molly said when the road suddenly deteriorated and her poor Camry started bouncing over potholes. She swerved to avoid the biggest ones, but there were just too many. Karen grabbed the handle over the door and braced herself against the center console to keep from getting jostled about.

"Are you sure?" Karen asked when five minutes later they were still bouncing.

"Sure about what?"

"Nothing. Sorry."

Another couple of minutes passed, and Molly flipped on her left turn signal. Karen studied the road ahead, but the trees were so thick that Molly had turned her headlights on. All of a sudden, she slowed down to a crawl. Karen didn't see any reason for it.

"What are we doing?"

"Did you see that big stump back there?"

Karen turned in her seat and looked through the back window. There was a pretty big stump on Molly's side of the road.

Molly said, "I know it's coming up when I see that stump."

"How many times have you been out here?"

Molly shrugged. "Not many. Half a dozen or so."

"And you know this guy from work?"

"From my old work. We were both at the Hazel Dell Library until they closed it. I got a job at Costco. He was at a hardware store for a while, the one on Burton, but I'm not sure what he does now."

"He knows we're coming, though, right?"

"John? Yeah. Why? Are you worried?"

Karen shrugged.

Molly laughed. "I agree his choice of place to live is... tedious? Cumbersome?"

"Inconvenient."

"Very. And, I'll warn you, he's a big bear of a guy. Big beard, hairy arms, the works. But he's a teddy, not a grizzly. He made Cole a wooden airplane a while back. Huge." She took her hands off the wheel and opened them three feet wide. "This big, at least. From scratch, too, not a kit. He's cool. And kind. You'll like him. We're here."

On the left side of Bullworth Drive, the trees parted just enough for a car to slip through. Karen wouldn't have noticed the dirt road had she been driving by herself because it was covered with bits of cedar fronds.

Looking closer, though, she saw tire marks.

The driveway was long, and then it just sort of ended. Karen had expected a clearing to open up, but it never did. The trees persisted, and at the last minute, a truck with a canopy came into view. Both the truck and its canopy were a green color that blended well with the forest, and the only reason Karen saw it was because of the glare of the Camry's headlights off the canopy's back window. Molly pulled up right behind it.

Karen looked around. There were trees all around them. "Are you going to have to back out of here?"

"No. It's tight and takes some doing, but I can turn around. Shall we go?"

Go where? Karen wanted to ask—there was nothing but trees—but she just said, "Yup," and got out of the car.

The air felt moist and smelled earthy, and the ground sucked at her feet, like it had recently rained. She crossed between the two vehicles and followed Molly up the driver's side of the truck.

In front of the truck was a giant cedar tree that ended the road. But beyond that was a footpath leading to the clearing Karen had been expecting. It was a tiny clearing. Barely big enough for the corrugated metal shack that was no bigger than a drive-thru-only coffee stand. There were cedar limbs lying on the ground at the foot of the shack. They looked like maybe they'd been stood up against it for camouflage, but had been blown down by the wind.

The two of them walked around the other side of the shack, and Karen was surprised to find a doorbell. Molly pushed it. Karen didn't hear anything but a light breeze rustling through the trees.

"Does he live underground?"

"Yup."

"Is he a prepper?"

"I don't think so. He's not hoarding for a rainy day. He just lives like it's a twenty-four/seven hurricane. What do you call that?"

"Prudent?"

A dim red light above the door turned on, and Karen heard a lock unlatch. Molly pulled open the rusty corrugated metal door.

But it was just a facade for something much thicker and stronger. Steel, maybe, about four inches thick. It looked homemade, too. There were welding lines along the door's edges.

In lieu of stairs, there was a ladder down a bright circular hole, and a pulley system for packages. Beside the hole was a simple bench made of light-colored wood, a rack for jackets, and a place for muddy shoes. A couple pairs of men's size twelves—work boots and rubber boots—were already sitting on the mat.

Molly slipped off her sneakers and then grabbed the top rung of the ladder and started making her descent.

Karen hadn't driven here herself. She wondered if now was the time to start regretting that fact. But either way, she figured that once Molly cleared the stairs, she really had no option but to climb down after her.

But as Molly reached the bottom, Karen heard a jolly baritone say, "Be right with you, Molly. I'm just finishing up a project."

"No worries."

Karen sighed instinctively, the exchange having touched something inside her that eased her concerns. She slipped off her shoes and set them next to Molly's, then climbed down the ladder.

After stepping through a vestibule, the bunker opened up into a cozy dome. It smelled faintly like cinnamon—real cinnamon, not chemical. The lighting was soft and welcoming, and the furnishings were warm, cozy and eclectic.

The dome was divided into four sections: a kitchenette that curved along the dome's wall to the left of the vestibule; a small bedroom separated from the rest of the dome by a passthrough bookcase filled with books, and a small walled-off section that

Karen assumed was a bathroom. The last section, to Karen's right, was a living space that included a couch, a storage ottoman, and a desk with several monitors, which was where John was seated.

"Make yourself at home," John said from his computer. "There's a pot of water on the back burner. Tea selections are on the counter."

Molly grabbed two coffee mugs from an upper cabinet like she'd done it before. The cups were a mismatched pair. One was white and said in a bold black font, *We didn't come this far to only go this far.* The other was yellow and showed a picture of Daffy Duck suffering some serious succotash.

Molly said, "He's got black pekoe, hibiscus, and oolong."

"Uh."

"Not a tea drinker?"

Karen shrugged.

"I think he's got some sugar." Molly pulled a handmade, glazed ceramic sugar bowl forward from the back of the counter and lifted its lid. "Yeah. Here. Do black pekoe. It's probably the most familiar, and it's got caffeine, so it's kind of like coffee. Add sugar if you need to."

The tea was loose leaf in glass jars. Karen copied Molly and spooned a scoop of black pekoe into a mesh strainer ball and hooked the chain onto her cup. Molly poured the water, and they took their steaming cups to the round table that was set up in front of the kitchenette.

"Almost there," John said.

Molly hadn't been lying. John was a big guy. Not overweight, per se, just big—tall, even sitting down, and thick with lots of hard-earned muscle. There was a lot of gray in his full head of light-brown hair. Molly put him in his mid-to-late fifties.

He hit a button on his keyboard and then pushed away from his desk, rolling across the smooth concrete floor to the table. He stuck his hand out to Karen.

"I'm John."

Karen accepted. His hand was warm and calloused. "I'm Karen. Thanks for having me."

"My pleasure. It's nice to meet you. Molly says you've seen some things."

Karen looked askance at Molly, wondering for a split second what Molly was up to, saying such things to strangers. But then she remembered this was precisely why they had come to Bullworth.

She told John about breaking the egg and then finding it whole again, about how she'd more or less confirmed it with surveillance video.

John nodded. "Sounds like Lemon Girl."

"Lemon... what?"

"Lemon Girl. She's a meme on the internet. She was working at a restaurant, cutting lemons, went to grab something off another counter, and when she came back to use the lemon she had just cut, it wasn't cut anymore."

"Seriously?"

"Just so. I can show you if you want."

"Yeah."

John rolled back to his computer desk, and Karen and Molly got up to follow him. His fingers worked quickly, taking them to a video-sharing site and then clicking on a search bar. He typed in the words *lemon girl glitch*.

The video he selected showed just what he had said: a girl cuts a lemon in half, then cuts it in half again. She grabs a plastic bag from another counter, goes to put the cut lemon half into the bag... and seems to notice it hasn't been cut. She pulls the lemon out of the bag, inspects it, and then picks up the knife and cuts it again.

Karen watched her do it all from a fairly straight-on camera angle.

"That's uncanny."

"It happens."

"Let me see it again."

John replayed the video. Karen watched for some kind of trick, but she didn't see anything questionable. The girl was wearing a blue apron and appeared to be at work. The kitchen was stainless steel and looked commercial. If the co-workers around her were movie extras, they were very good.

Karen said, "It hasn't been debunked?"

"Oh, sure. People say she didn't cut it all the way through, that cut lemons can stick together, that the video was edited, tons of explanations. There's a mentalist who recreated the shot to debunk it, but the first cut *he* makes is shown awfully fast and probably *doesn't* cut all the way through. He also cuts it end to end, and he doesn't try to pull the lemon apart."

John rewound the video and paused it, then made the video bigger.

"Lemon Girl cut across the middle—see?—not end to end. If it was cut at all, even with the thinnest knife blade, there would have been a cut line. So even if the halves were stuck together, she would've seen the cut line and pulled the halves apart and gone on with whatever she was doing. She's at work. Why wouldn't she? And really, that's what she does anyway: she cuts the lemon again and gets on with the job. But look at her face."

He pointed at the girl's face as she cut the lemon in half a second time. She was looking off to the side like *What the fu…? Am I the only person witnessing this?*

Karen knew that emotion. She'd expressed it herself when she'd found her cracked egg whole again.

"You sound like you've watched this a few times," she said.

"You bet I have."

Karen had been half joking, and John's earnestness took her aback. She straightened up and stepped away from him.

"I keep record of these things," John said. "I have a special fondness for the ones that evidence seems to support. But for me, it's not about whether the lemon was actually cut. To me, it's about why the world gives people so many opportunities to *wonder* if the lemon was actually cut. Or if the egg was really cracked."

"Or how the shower knob is suddenly fixed."

"Come again?"

"That same day, the egg day—yesterday, I guess—the knob in the shower all of a sudden worked differently."

"For the better?"

"Yeah. It used to turn on hot water right away, but with low pressure. It's been like that for years, since we moved in. Paul and I always said we should fix it, but we never have. Then yesterday it goes cold to hot, and hot has really nice pressure. I thought Paul fixed it, but he says he didn't. I know *I* didn't fix it."

"Anything else happen that day?"

"Like what?"

"Nothing in particular."

"No, *something* in particular. What?"

"Anything. Something more. A third glitch. It could be anything."

Karen thought of the flickers. But they didn't feel the same as the egg incident. They felt silly. Not as compelling. She shrugged and shook her head.

"Well, keep your eye out," John said. "I bet you see something else."

Karen glanced at Molly, who was standing silently behind John's other shoulder, volleying back and forth with the conversation.

Molly said, "Do you know what a glitch is?"

"A glitch?" Karen's gaze traveled to the last word John had entered into the search bar when he'd searched for the lemon girl video: *lemon girl glitch*.

"Tell her about glitches," Molly said.

"Glitches?" John said, and he turned to Karen. "A glitch in the matrix—like the movie. Have you seen the movie?"

"Sure," Karen said.

But thinking of the film brought up images of sleek actors in even sleeker black outfits fighting agents in slow-motion and anti-gravity, all in dark, gritty settings. It was a great movie. But it felt like the complete opposite of a suburban T-ball mom's brownie-baking and shower conundrums.

John said, "The glitch in that movie is the black cat, the deja vu. But a glitch can be anything that happens that suggests we're not living in a purely physical world. If it were a purely physical world, and you cut a lemon or cracked an egg, it's not going back together without glue and someone's effort. And even when it's fixed, there would still be cracks that'll show it had once been in pieces. In a truly physical world, nothing could go back together all by itself and with no evidence of damage, like nothing had ever happened to it."

Karen nodded, but the idea was still at best a vague concept in her mind and not an understanding.

And she hadn't seen any deja vu.

"So you've seen more of these, then, these glitches?" she asked John.

"I've experienced a few. Seen a few on video. Heard of a lot more. But anyone truly interested usually keeps it to themselves."

"Because of the ridicule?"

"That, sure. For some. But for others, they couldn't care less what others think. They keep it to themselves because the glitch is just the beginning. It's hard enough to get yourself to the other side of understanding without trying to pull the heel-dragging disbelievers along with you."

"Is that you?" Karen asked. "Someone who's trying to get to the other side of understanding?"

John looked up at her, his honest honey-brown eyes drawing her back toward him. "That's me."

"Are you there yet? To the other side?"

"Nah," John said with a grin that revealed straight white teeth hidden in that beard of his. "I'm still searching. My map's getting better, though. My compass, too."

Karen wanted to ask him about what he'd seen, but she didn't figure he'd tell her. She'd already asked him for examples of other glitches, and he hadn't given her any. But that was fine. She could google.

"You said something about the world making us wonder?"

John nodded. "I think the world uses glitches to get us to question what we're told about it, about reality."

Karen shook her head. "Why would the world do that?"

"To get us talking. To get us thinking."

"Okay, but why would the world want us to question it? Why would the world care?"

"Why do you assume it wouldn't care?"

Karen didn't have an answer.

"I think it cares deeply," John said. "I think it's telling us things. It just has a different communication style than we're used to."

"Glitches?"

"They happen. People report them. Too often for us to just ignore them all. And some of those people bring receipts." He tapped the lemon-girl video. "So why are so many *other* people so adamant for us to dismiss these things outright? Why are they so angry about us asking questions? You should read some of the doubters and debunkers. I hope you like vitriol."

"I can imagine." Karen crossed her arms and stood quietly, trying to wrap her brain around the point of all this.

"What?" John said.

Karen glanced at him. He was nice, and she didn't want to be rude.

But John was perceptive. "I'm an old guy, and aside from knowing your name is Karen, I don't know you from Eve. There's not much you can say to me that can hurt my feelings. So out with it."

"This is all very interesting."

"But?"

"But I don't know how it helps me. I don't know why I'm here. I mean, thank you for bringing me," she said to Molly. "I'm not sorry I came. And I'm actually really liking this tea. But... I guess I'm not getting the point."

"You saw two glitches," John said. "Yes?"

"Yes."

"In one day?"

"Yeah."

"Is that not odd to you?"

"It is odd. It's very odd. Isn't it odd?"

"It's odd," John said, "to a newbie."

"Meaning?"

"Glitches are just the beginning."

"So I should expect more?"

John nodded.

"More glitches?"

"To start."

"And then what?"

"And then the world communicating with you won't seem like such an odd notion. And then you'll be open to more. And then you'll come back here."

Chapter 5

"Have you ever seen a glitch?" Karen asked Molly on the drive back to Starbucks, where her car was parked.

Molly said, "Not personally. But I was working at the library with John when he first experienced his."

"What was it? If you don't mind my asking."

"I don't mind. He said he kept seeing sets of three people who looked exactly the same doing the same thing. Three old white-haired women with red cardigans and denim ankle-length skirts sleeping in different seats on the left side of the bus. Three men in the same plaid shirt with the same level of baldness standing in the same spot, just outside the candy rack, in three separate checkout lines at the grocery store. Three little boys in the same striped shirt and shorts, each holding a basketball—although he thought that one could just be a set of biological triplets."

"Really?"

"It's what he said."

"That is kind of weird. That's a glitch?"

"Some think so."

"But you don't?"

"It sounds more like a coincidence to me. But he went online to see if anyone else had experienced anything like that, and he found people who had. And to me, *that* felt like more than just a coincidence. That felt meaningful."

"Meaningful how?"

"I guess just as he said. It got people talking."

That night, after putting the kids to bed, Karen sat on the edge of her own king-sized bed to floss. Paul was lounging against the headboard, pointing the remote at the TV as he searched for something to watch.

Karen said, "You know Molly?"

"The woman from T-ball yesterday?"

"Yeah. She took me to meet this old underground-bunker guy today."

"Like a real bunker?"

"Yeah. Except without all the guns and prepper stuff. It was kind of nice, actually. Even with no windows. It was like this warm and cozy dome. Anyway, he said the egg thing and the shower-knob thing—he called them glitches."

"What's a glitch?"

"Glitches in the matrix—like the movie. He says it's anything that makes you question the physicality of reality."

"Deep."

"Shut up." Grinning, Karen swatted Paul's foot.

Paul laughed. "So what else did he say?"

Karen told Paul everything she could remember about her conversation with John.

"Anyway," she said, "he said that I should expect to see more."

"More glitches?"

Karen nodded.

"How do you make them happen?"

"What?"

"Glitches. How do you make more happen?"

That's what Karen had *thought* Paul had said, and the notion had her stopping mid-floss to imagine the possibilities.

"What?" Paul asked.

"John didn't say anything about making glitches happen. But what if we could?"

"Can you?"

"I don't know."

But Karen woke up the next morning feeling certain she could. And that afternoon, she got to the school's pick-up corner early to talk to Molly.

To Karen's delight, Molly was already there when she arrived.

"Hey," she said, tugging on Molly's sleeve. "I wanted to ask you something."

"What's up?"

Karen beckoned Molly further down the sidewalk, away from the tut-tutters. Glitch pros might be able to brush off ridicule from non-believers like water from a duck, but Karen wasn't there yet.

"What's up?" Molly asked again.

Karen peeked around her to make sure none of the parents still standing on the sidewalk corner were listening. They weren't; a couple squirrels racing around the metal railing had captured their attention. Karen whispered to Molly, "Can I *make* a glitch happen?"

"I don't know. Do you want to ask John?"

"Kind of, but I wanted to ask you first. I don't want to bug him. He was super nice, but also kind of playing it close to the chest, you know? But I get it. He wants me to do the work. And that makes sense. If I do the work, then I'm the real deal, not someone who's just listening now so I can debunk and ridicule later. But I don't want to just watch and wait and always be asking myself, Is that a glitch? Is *that* a glitch? I want to make one happen. If I can. I want to make a glitch happen. I just don't know how to do it. Do you know how to do it?"

"Not offhand."

"Okay." Karen sighed and turned to walk back to the corner. "Just thought I'd ask."

"Well, hang on. I don't know off the top of my head. But that doesn't mean we can't figure it out. Right?"

"How do we figure it out?"

"It's the universe," Molly said. "The world," she clarified when Karen frowned at the word *universe*. "John says 'world,' but I like 'universe.' To me, 'world' includes all the people in all of their nefarious incarnations. But the 'universe' is big and powerful enough to break through to us despite what other people do. I don't know. Maybe it's silly. Doesn't matter. World, universe. Point is, if the universe is going to communicate with you, it's going to use something you already know. It's not going to make you go learn math or some complicated thing, despite what the world tells us. It's not going to make you spend years learning something new in order to understand it eventually. It's going to communicate with you now using what you already now know. So what do we know?"

Karen shook her head. "I don't know."

"Well," Molly said, "we know a glitch is something that makes us wonder, something that makes us question, because it's something unexpected."

"Okay... so?"

"*So*... as above, so below. If you want to see and experience the unexpected, *be* unexpected."

Chapter 6

Be unexpected

Be *un*expected.

Be unexpected.

What did it mean to be unexpected?

And unexpected to whom?

Karen stopped at the first red light out of the school's neighborhood and looked in the rearview mirror.

Lila and Kyle were strapped into their booster seats, quietly looking out their windows. She and Paul had gotten lucky. So far, her kids had gotten along together awfully well. Karen and Paul often wondered if the serenity would last. Karen had her doubts. She couldn't recall any serenity with her own brother. Then again, they had *always* been at each other when they were younger, starting long before they'd gotten to be Kyle and Lila's age.

"Did anything unexpected happen at school today?" she asked them.

Neither of her kids said anything right away. Karen couldn't really see Lila. But Kyle, seated on the passenger side, made a face.

"Anything unexpected happen at recess?" she asked him.

"I found a frog."

"That's cool. Where'd you find it?"

"On the grass."

"What did you do with it?"

"We made it a house."

"That was nice of you. What did you use?"

"Leaves and stuff."

"Nice," Karen said. "Anything else happen that was unexpected?"

Kyle shrugged.

"What about you, Lila? Anything unexpected happen today?"

"I found three dimes."

"Yeah? All together or separately?"

"I don't know what that means."

"Did you find three dimes in the same spot, or did you find one dime, and then later another dime, and then later another?"

"I found two in the hallway and one on my desk."

"*On* your desk?"

"Yeah."

"That *is* unexpected."

"Yeah. And then Mr. Ramseth talked about dimes."

"Today?"

"Yeah. After I found the one on my desk."

"It wasn't there when you got to class this morning?"

"No."

"Really?"

"Yeah. It was there after lunch."

"Did Mr. Ramseth put it there?"

"I don't know."

"What did he say about dimes?"

"Math problems and stuff, with money."

"Like counting change?"

"I guess."

"Did you use real dimes?"

"No. Just on the board."

"So the dime wasn't from using dimes in class?"

"No."

"Huh."

Lila was getting annoyed—Karen could tell by her tone—so Karen left off with asking her any more questions. Although, she wanted to ask if Lila herself had found it strange about all the dimes. Because the way she talked about it, it didn't sound like she did. It sounded like she thought it had all made for just another average day.

Karen wasn't sure whether the dime thing was a glitch or a mere coincidence or what. It kind of sounded like John's triple-sightings glitch, with all the look-a-like people all dressed the same way and found in the same spot. Finding triplets of things wasn't as satisfying a glitch as the egg thing or the shower fix. But was finding triplets unexpected? Karen figured it was, in the sense that no one expects to find anything in particular, let alone three of the same somethings.

But was it *really* unexpected? People drop money all the time. And a lot of times they don't stoop to pick it up. So did a thing being explainable undermine its unexpectedness?

Karen got the kids home and seated at the kitchen table doing their homework.

Homework in the early grades of elementary. And every day, too. At the very least, a work sheet. And outside, it just kept getting darker and darker earlier and earlier. No time to play.

But Karen couldn't complain about it too much. The homework kept the kids busy for a spell.

As she made dinner, she thought about the dime on Lila's desk: *That* was definitely unexpected, even if Mr. Ramseth had put it there—because why would he do that? If you had a dime in your hand, why wouldn't you just put in your pocket? Or add it to a change jar?

But mostly, Karen thought about being unexpected.

Causing more unexpected things to happen to her was the goal. More unexpected *fixes,* preferably. Like the shower. That would be amazing. The house had all sorts of little busted and odd things about it that could use a little magic fairy dust.

But how could Karen cause the fixes to happen? Why had she received the shower fix in the first place?

How was she supposed to be unexpected?

And unexpected for whom?

After putting the kids to bed, she sat on the edge of her own bed with her dental floss while Paul was watching TV.

"How can I be unexpected?"

Paul started pulling at his boxers. "You want to be unexpected right now?"

She rolled her eyes at him.

"It *would* be unexpected," he said, waiting a hopeful beat before settling back against the headboard.

Karen snorted and shook her head—but then she thought of something, something sparked by Paul's completely expected behavior. She pointed at him and said, "Actually, no. Thank you. That was helpful. To cause a glitch, Molly told me to be unexpected. Okay, sure. But how do you be unexpected? And unexpected for whom?"

"Not for me, apparently."

"Right. So, unexpected for whom?"

Paul stared at the TV, not answering.

Karen went into the bathroom thinking the conversation was over. She brushed her teeth, washed her face.

But when she came back out again, Paul said, "You said you're trying to get the world to glitch, right? That the world is communicating with you?"

"Right."

"So do something that's unexpected to the world."

"To the world..." she said. "Like what?"

"I don't know. You're the glitch master."

"I am, aren't I?"

She totally wasn't. She had no idea what she could do that would surprise the world.

But she knew where she could start. "And if it would be unexpected to you, it *might* also be unexpected to the world."

Paul nodded hopefully.

She gave him the look and climbed up onto the bed.

Chapter 7

The next day was a Saturday. The sun rose late, but it rose warm and shining in a bright blue sky. Karen and Paul made the kids French toast and then took them out to the park on the waterfront. It wasn't something they usually did, but Karen couldn't say for sure whether that necessarily made it unexpected.

Turned out that, nope, their adventure definitely did not qualify as unexpected. Not to Karen's mind, anyway. Not if a whole lot of other people had also had the same idea.

The park was crowded with people out in jeans and hoodies enjoying one of the year's last good-weather days. Paul and Karen strolled along the boardwalk that ran along the river while the kids rode their bikes back and forth in the bike lane.

They were walking slowly enough that Karen pulled out her phone.

"Who you calling?" Paul asked.

"No one. I'm checking something."

Paul kept watch on the kids and on the foot traffic, tugging Karen out of the way of passersby as needed.

Karen said, "Have you heard of Nelson Mandela?"

"I think so. South African guy? Went to prison, got out and became president?"

"Yeah. Some people remember him dying in prison."

"Well, if he became president, how did he do that?"

"I don't know. He died in 2013, but some people remember him dying in the eighties."

"Some people meaning who?"

"Just people. What do you mean?"

"I wasn't alive in the eighties," Paul said. "Neither were you. So whether he died then or not, we wouldn't remember either way. We weren't here yet."

Karen looked up at him. "It's interesting you say that. From what I've been reading, things like the Mandela thing—where people remember events and brands being different from how they are—people say these kinds of glitches happen because something about reality has changed—but it's not a clean change. There's a rippling effect. It leaves traces."

"So he died, and then something changed, making it so that he couldn't be dead anymore?"

"I guess."

"Weird."

"Yeah. But if the change to reality happened in, say, 1990, we'd remember it the new way, but people born before that, in the early eighties or whatever, they'd probably remember it the old way."

"One way to find out," Paul said, veering them off the path.

"What are we doing?" Karen asked.

"Excuse me?" Paul said, approaching an elderly group of people gathered around a table outside a coffee shop along the boardwalk. "Can you help settle a bet for us? My wife and I can't agree about when Mandela died."

"Nelson Mandela?" said the lone elderly guy. He was sitting with his back to the wall in the center of a group of elderly women, reminding Karen of a king holding court. "He died in the eighties. What was it? Eighty-seven?"

"I think that sounds about right," said one of the women. "The procession was on the news. His widow gave a speech."

"That she did. Wore a hat," said the man.

"You *remember* that?" said another woman. "I thought I remembered that, too, but then I saw in the paper he died in the early twenty-tens."

"2013?" Karen asked.

"Could be," said the woman.

"No, it was 1987," said the man. "I've got a memory like a vise grip."

"I tell you, it was more recent than that. It was in the paper."

An argument was brewing. Paul grabbed Karen and started backing away, saying, "I guess that means our bet's still open. Thank you kindly, everyone."

Paul and Karen hurried down the boardwalk, away from the group. Karen waited to get out of earshot to say, "Well, that was weird. Even the woman who read he died in 2013 said she'd thought he'd died in the eighties."

"Eighty-seven."

"Whatever. That guy was pretty adamant, though, wasn't he? No one's changing his mind that it wasn't eighty-seven. Why do some people trust themselves and others readily agree that their memory is just faulty?"

"Evidence," Paul said. "It was in the paper."

"Like *that* makes anything true. And I don't think seeing it in the paper now is going to change *that* guy's mind."

"Point taken. But it's common knowledge the memory is

faulty. The mind is susceptible to confabulation, suggestibility, confirmation bias, plausibility bias. Ask me how I know."

"I'm good, Mr. Prosecutor; I know how you know. And *susceptible* doesn't mean *foregone conclusion*."

"Hey, Mom," Lila said, riding her bike up to them, Kyle racing after her. "Can we go jump in the bounce house?"

Lila stopped, planted a foot, and pointed back down the boardwalk. The city, or someone, had set up a blue-and-red striped inflatable house with black mesh walls.

"Sure."

"You guys need money?" Paul asked. He dug into his pocket and pulled out some cash. A coin fell with a clang on the sidewalk. Karen picked it up.

It was a dime.

Paul gave Lila a ten-dollar bill. "For your brother, too, okay? Go ahead. We'll meet you there."

They raced off.

Karen flashed Paul the dime.

"What?" he said. "Did I drop that."

"Yup. It's a dime."

Paul tried to take it, but Karen held it away.

"What? What are you doing?" Paul asked.

Karen showed him the dime again. "Lila was telling me about all these dimes she found yesterday, about how Mr. Ramseth had then talked about dimes."

"And now you've found a dime?"

"And now I've found a dime."

"I dropped it," Paul said.

"You did. I saw you. Does that make it any less meaningful?"

"Kind of."

"Why?"

"I don't know."

"But it does, doesn't it?"

 Paul shrugged a yes.

"Like the math."

"What?"

"The world makes it seem like only super smart and educated people, like people great at math and physics and quantum mechanics and whatever, can understand the world."

"Sounds like church," Paul said. "You gotta go because only the priests or whoever can understand God."

"Right? But Molly says it's not actually like that. She says the universe uses what we know to communicate with us." Karen bumped shoulders with Paul. "So maybe it also uses *who* we know."

Chapter 8

"Let's be unexpected," Karen said when they got back to the car.

"I liked being unexpected last night," Paul whispered with a grin.

"No, I mean, let's take a weird way home or go somewhere new."

"Like where?"

"Wherever. You guys want to go for a drive?"

"Yeah!"

"Yay!" Karen echoed, flashing Paul a three-against-one grin. She checked that Kyle was buckled into his booster while Paul stuffed the bikes in the back. They met back up in the front seat.

Karen leaned across the center console. "So, driver, where are you taking us?"

"How should I know?" Paul said as he turned on the car. "It's gonna be unexpected."

Karen kissed him on the cheek. "Perfect."

Paul pulled the SUV away from the curb and moved into traffic. Karen tapped the screen on the dash. They usually listened to a music streaming service, so she turned on the radio and scanned for something different.

Talk radio… rock… country… classical—

"*What* is *this*?" Lila said from the back seat.

It was a guy singing opera.

"I think you've found your unexpected radio," Paul said.

So Karen sat back and listened. She'd never been to the opera. But she imagined the four of them dressed in swanky outfits sitting in red seats in the front row of the balcony with their little spectacle glasses and an excellent view of the baritone strutting around on stage.

At the light where they usually turned right onto Cornell, Paul turned left towards the more commercial part of town.

"Where are you going?"

"You said to be unexpected."

"Oh, right."

"Guess I succeeded. Is that not what you want to do?"

"No, it is."

Karen shook her head, wondering how she'd forgotten the assignment so quickly—her own assignment, too. Odd.

But it just got odder. She suddenly had a feeling like she shouldn't be doing what they were doing, like she should be at home doing laundry or prepping for the week to come.

"Is there anything else we have to do this weekend?" she asked.

Paul shrugged and took a right off of Cornell, down a street they'd never had reason to visit before. The fast food chains gave way to what looked like doctors' offices.

"I'd like to catch the game tomorrow," he said. "It's a division game, so it matters."

"Does it?"

The radio DJ came on, and a calming, sultry voice told them they were listening to "Largo al Factotum" from *The Barber of Seville*.

"Hey, look," Karen said, pointing out the window at a storefront with a red-white-and-blue-spiraled pole out front. "There's a barber! I didn't know we had a barber."

Paul said, "Is that a kind of glitch?"

"What's a barber?" Lila asked.

Karen said, "It's an old-fashioned place to get a shave and a haircut."

"Oh."

Lila sounded disappointed. Karen pulled down her sun visor to check on Kyle in the mirror. He was starting to mess with his seat buckle.

"Let's head back," she said to Paul.

"Sounds good."

Back home, Karen sat on the couch with her laptop while Paul and the kids were out in the backyard.

Acting unexpected probably wasn't something she'd be able to keep doing during family time. Paul and the kids just weren't into it like she was. They were tolerant, but not interested. And Karen didn't want to take advantage of her family's tolerance. So she was going to have to be more purposeful about all this so that she could fit it in on the weekdays when she was alone.

She'd already looked up what kinds of things people considered a type of glitch: deja vu; objects disappearing and reappearing in weird places; identical strangers, like John's triple sightings. There were other things, too. Lots more, in fact. But Karen had only taken special note of the ones that she herself had experienced personally. The ones that had resonated.

Except for the Mandela Effect, the name given to the phenomenon of people remembering things being different from how they now were. Karen had taken note of that one.

She didn't really have an opinion about most of the examples. She didn't remember Nelson Mandela at all, let alone dying, regardless of the date of his death. Nor was she familiar with the Fruit of the Loom label, whether it was the current one or the one that some people swore used to include a cornucopia. And she didn't remember ever seeing most of the movies with famous but misremembered quotes; she only remembered having heard people (mis)quote them.

But she was a mid-Millennial. It struck her as odd that most of these changes were remembered differently depending on when you were born. It was mostly Gen Xers and older generations, and some of the elder Millennials, who remembered things being different.

And no wonder. The vast majority of contested brands were at their peak of popularity in the eighties. The contested events were fewer, but they, too, largely had their original instances happen somewhere in the eighties.

But there were some outliers that stood out to Karen. Like the Pokemon character Pikachu. Karen didn't have an opinion either way, but some people swore that the character's tail, which was yellow, used to have a black tip. Karen noted this example because Pikachu wasn't introduced until 1996.

Also interesting? And Karen herself remembered this one. People say there was a movie in the nineties called *Shazaam*, starring Sinbad as a genie. Karen could see the actor in her mind, wearing a cropped vest and blackish-gold harem pants.

And yet there was no such movie. There was, however, a movie Karen had never heard of until now called *Kazaam*, starring Shaquille O'Neal as a genie, and it came out in 1996.

The internet was ramping up in 1996. And the internet itself told Karen that it was the reason why people misremembered things from the past. But that made no sense to Karen. If people hadn't been connected by the internet back then, and they were all just be-bopping along in their own little communities, then how did they all remember the same details in the same wrong way?

Blaming the power of suggestion for all of this misremembering didn't work for Karen, either. People don't remember things happening just because someone suggests they happened—and thank goodness. Her kids would've found plenty of ways to use that loophole on her and Paul if mere suggestion worked that way. But it doesn't. And when people don't remember something the way it's being suggested, they push back—as evidenced by all the people pushing back because they couldn't remember something being any other way than how it currently was. And, really, why *wouldn't* they push back? When people first encounter the Mandela Effect, they have no idea what it is. They have no stake in it. They're just telling what they remember.

Karen opened her laptop and pulled out her list of things she'd heard John and Molly mention that she still didn't fully understand and had missed asking about at the time.

Things like John asking if the weird change to her shower was for the better. At the time, Karen had just answered the question. But it was a question based on an assumption. John had assumed that whatever had happened, it had been good. Why had he done that? He could have assumed that it had been bad, or he could have made no assumptions at all—that's what Karen would have done. So what made John assume, correctly, that the change was good?

It could be something as simple as the observation that things in the world—man-made things, anyway—usually break down. So only good things happening—man-made things getting better for no discernible reason—would be noteworthy as odd. Karen suspected there might be something more to John's assumption than this, but this answer satisfied her for now.

John had also mentioned the physical world. He'd said that glitches suggest we're not living in a physical world. But if the world wasn't physical, then what kind of world was it? Karen thought she'd come up with some decent answers for that one, too, depending on one's preferred discipline. The world was spiritual or it was vibrational.

Or maybe it was both.

A few questions on her list still had no answers despite all her thinking about them. For example, John kept saying that the glitch was just the beginning. Well then, what happened after a glitch? And what was the end game?

But first, Karen started with an easier question. She opened a browser and typed in the search bar *Why do they call a glitch a 'glitch in the matrix'?*

The AI overview at the top of the page told her it was because the idea of glitches was an extension of the idea that reality is a computer simulation.

Below that, she found mention in the search results of a documentary by the same name.

But before she could dig further into her results, the French doors to her right opened up and the troops stomped in, brushing the bottoms of their shoes off on the mat. They'd been working in Paul's little garden, pulling weeds or whatever they did; Karen didn't know. Her thumb was not green.

Karen closed the laptop and set it aside. "Done already?"

"It's raining," Paul said.

He and the kids peeled off their coats and sweatshirts and Paul hung them up on a rack behind the front door. Outside, the sun shined brightly through the light sprinkling of drops.

They made snacks, and then Lila said she was going to go see what a friend was doing down the street. That inspired Kyle to want to go see a friend, too, so Karen called the friend's mom to make arrangements, and she and Paul drove Kyle over to the house. On the way back, they used a coupon to pick up a couple take-and-bake pizzas for dinner.

At a light, Karen said, "You want to watch a movie with me?"

"Now?"

"Yeah, while the kids are gone. Why? What did you want to do?"

"I was kind of hoping we could be unexpected again."

Karen sighed for effect. "*Fine*—and then we watch a movie. Deal?"

"Deal."

When the light turned green, the SUV was suddenly traveling a little faster. Karen didn't mind. She almost told Paul to take it faster still. Maybe she'd yank on the wheel or inch her foot past the center console and into his footwell so that when Paul inevitably slowed for a yellow light, she could unexpectedly slam her foot on the gas.

Chapter 9

"What movie are we watching?" Paul said as he found the remote and lounged back against the headboard.

Karen went into the bathroom. "It's a documentary," she said. "Go to the library app."

As she flushed, Paul said, "What's it called?"

"*A Glitch in the Matrix.*"

A few seconds later, Karen heard an unfamiliar voice talking on the TV.

"Hey, pause it," she said. "Wait for me."

The TV voice went quiet.

Karen finished up and stepped out of the bathroom. She grabbed up all of the free pillows and piled them up against the headboard on her side of the bed. Then she went downstairs to get a glass of water, came back up. She set the water by the bed and then searched for the throw blanket that had gotten knocked off onto the floor.

She caught a whiff of something in the air. She sniffed. "Do you smell that?"

"What?"

"Smells like a fire."

"Did you use the toaster?"

"No. You don't smell it?"

She went to the window. They often slept with it open at night and had sometimes smelled weed, but never a fire.

"Is it open?" Paul asked.

"Yeah, but it's pouring outside. You don't smell it? It's like a campfire after the flames die down."

Paul liked to camp and his favorite part was the fire, so she knew the smell. It always came home with them on their clothes.

When Paul didn't answer she turned to look at him. "Like a campfire," she said again. "You don't smell it?"

He had a weird look on his face.

"You okay?"

He raised his eyebrows and pointed at the TV.

The movie was paused and the screen was black. But in the center of the black screen were three words: *A Campfire Production*.

"Well, that's creepy," Karen said. "You don't smell it?"

But as she said it, the smell started to fade. She sniffed the air. "I don't smell it anymore."

Clutching the blanket, she climbed onto the bed and snuggled in closer to Paul than she'd been intending to do. "Should we still watch it?"

"I kind of think we have to. Don't you?"

"Hit it," she said.

Paul pushed play, and right away, they learned that the guy talking over the title cards was named Paul.

"Okay, this just keeps getting weirder," Paul said.

But he didn't pick up the remote or get up to leave, so Karen figured he was okay to keep watching.

But as the talking guy named Paul came on the screen, and

the interviewer started asking him about something called *simulation theory*—and Karen's Paul explained to her that documentary-Paul's CGI appearance was an *avatar*—the phone rang.

Kyle needed someone to come get him.

Karen and Paul turned off the documentary and went together to go pick him up.

"Do you know anything about simulation theory?" Karen asked Paul in the car.

"I've heard of it before," he said. "I think I saw something once where Elon Musk was saying we're living in a computer game. That we're all just characters—avatars—being shuttled around by some higher intelligence. Something like that."

"Do you think he's right?"

"I don't know. I don't *feel* like I'm really the skin of some gamer in his mom's basement."

"Yeah, me neither. I feel like I'm in control."

Kyle was fine; it was just that the fort he and his friend had built with couch cushions had fallen over on him while he was inside.

"And it scared him, that's all," said the friend's mom.

"Well, thanks for calling," Paul said.

Karen took Kyle by the hand and got him settled in the SUV's back seat.

"You okay, buddy?"

Kyle nodded, but he was sucking his thumb. She hadn't seen him do that in a couple years. She ruffled his hair. "We'll get you home, okay?"

Back in the front seat, she called the house Lila was at to check on her. She was fine. In fact, she and her friend had decided to have a sleepover.

"We've got everything she might need," the mom said. "And I'll have her fed before I send her home in the morning."

"Sounds good. Have a great night." It was the usual routine.

Back home, Kyle was pooped, so they got him ready for bed.

"You want to finish that documentary?" Paul said when they were back in bed themselves.

"Nah," Karen said. "I've had enough of the unexpected."

But Karen had just been tired.

The next morning, she was back on the laptop, asking a chatbot about simulation theory.

She went down a rabbit hole that brought up holograms and the double-slit experiment, an experiment first conducted in 1801, over two hundred years ago. It suggested that the world behaves differently depending on whether someone is watching.

Both holograms and the double-slit experiment had something to do with a concept called *pattern interference*. At least, that was one of the bolded phrases that stuck out to Karen. She wasn't all that science savvy and was mostly just skimming the bot's answers for bolded words that sounded interesting.

She asked the bot if glitches had anything to do with pattern interference.

She didn't get an answer right away. The cursor rotated, and then an error message popped up: *You've been signed out. Please sign in again to use this chatbot.*

Karen stared at the message. She'd used this chatbot several times before now, and never once had she ever signed in. So why was it telling her she'd been signed out, that she had to sign in again?

She hit the browser's refresh button instead.

The window refreshed, and she retyped her question into the chatbot: *How are glitches in the matrix related to interference patterns?*

She got the same error message.

"Hey, Paul?" He was watching football next to her on the couch in the downstairs family room. Lila was still at her friend's house, and Kyle was making something out of building bricks on the floor. "Any idea why this chatbot is telling me to sign in? I've never signed in. It's told me twice I need to sign in."

"What are you doing?"

"Asking about whether glitches have anything to do with interference patterns."

"And what's your computer doing?"

"Giving me an error message. It's done it twice now."

Grinning, Paul said, "Sounds like it's glitching."

"What?"

Paul shrugged. "Well, doesn't it?"

Karen looked back at the error message. It was just a simple white rectangular message with rounded edges and a black outline—and she'd never seen one like it before, in appearance or message.

"A computer glitch," she said, mostly to herself.

But Paul said, "What did you think they meant by simulation theory? It's using computers as a metaphor for reality."

His team fumbled, and he yelled at the screen, then got up to get something from the kitchen.

Using the same chatbot—and receiving no error message this time—she asked it how to make a computer glitch.

As far as she could tell, not being all that computer savvy, the gist of the answer was that she had to overwhelm the system.

Computers only had so much processing power. So if you asked it to do more than the processor could handle, it would glitch.

"What was that you were saying about the video game thing?" she asked Paul when he came back with a small plate of apples and cheese. "Something about how we're all supposedly characters being played by someone else?"

"Just that, I guess. We wake up when they log in as us."

She shook her head, still not buying the idea. But she did a little more research, and by halftime she had her own idea.

Simulation theory seemed to suggest that the world didn't constantly exist. Instead, it postulated that the world was rendered on an as-needed basis. If no one was using it or looking at it, then details—stuff and even whole places—disappeared until they were needed again.

The theory offered a similar idea about people.

Likening the world to a game, it suggested that not everyone was a real player with a consciousness. Some people were just there for decoration. In this way, they fulfilled a necessary but limited function that required less processing power.

These ideas didn't resonate with Karen.

For one, it just didn't sound right to her that some people weren't fully realized. Could she prove it? No. But her gut told her that the assumption was wrong. To her it just seemed like a convenient way to label some people as less than human.

For two, she didn't buy the idea that the universe had finite processing power. Just because humans were limited and the things that they made (like computers) were limited, didn't make the universe limited. To her, this hypothesis sounded like typical scientific arrogance. There were a lot of things humanity still didn't know about the universe, and yet we still had a tendency to conclude that if we didn't understand something (yet), it was because the thing in question was just irrelevant junk.

That said, even if the universe did have infinite processing power, that didn't mean it couldn't get used to giving only the amount of power that was usually needed, that it couldn't be surprised by a sudden surge in need.

And she could also get behind the idea that at any given time, you never had everyone on the planet maxing out their needs for processing power. Because at any given time, a third of the world, give or take, was asleep.

So theoretically, if you could spontaneously wake everyone in the world up at the same time and immediately get them focusing on something that maxed out their brain and body powers, that might overwhelm the world enough to cause it to glitch. In a massive way, too.

But that kind of worldwide cooperation wasn't ever likely to happen. Nor was it anything Karen was going to be able to do by herself. Not to mention, you'd probably only get one shot at it before the universe copped wise and started making more power more readily available.

Still, the idea of using a computer glitch as a metaphor for causing her own glitch intrigued her.

What might she do to overwhelm the rendering of her own life experience?

Chapter 10

That night Karen woke up from the weirdest dream.

"I was lucid," she told Paul, after finding that he wasn't asleep either. The two of them were now cuddled up together under a blanket in their chair-and-a-half, which they'd nudged a few degrees so that it would face the main floor's front window. They were still dressed in their pajamas, the kids still asleep. Only the tiny light above the range in the kitchen behind them was on. They sipped their coffee from their matching pale-yellow law school mugs and stared out at the shadows cast by the streetlights and the front yard's big oak tree. "Have you ever had a lucid dream?"

"Yeah, once or twice."

"You know how you can do anything?" Karen said. "Fly. Teleport from one place to another. You can do anything when you're lucid. Right?"

"Yeah, as far as I remember. It's been a while."

"I couldn't do anything like that," Karen said. "I couldn't even choose to walk a little faster. I was walking in slow motion, like I was wading through molasses and experiencing drag. I knew I was dreaming, and yet I was more stuck, I had less willpower, less... I don't know what I'm trying to say."

"No, I get it. You were lucid. And when you're lucid, you're supposed to be powerful. But you had even less power than normal."

"Yes," she said, shivers rising up her arms. "That exactly."

She set her mug down on her armrest tray and started untangling herself from the blanket.

"I'm gonna grab a banana or something. You want anything?"

"Nah"

She found the end of the blanket and whipped it off her—and hit her mug of coffee. It crashed to the floor, shattering into pieces and spilling coffee all over the hardwoods.

"No! I love that mug!"

She carefully got to her feet.

Paul got up, too, and flipped on the light, then headed into the kitchen. He came back with a towel. "Here," he said, handing her the towel. "I'll check the kids."

Karen used the towel to push the mess into a pile. She knelt down beside it and started gathering up the bigger pieces of broken mug.

This mug was—had been—her graduation mug. When she and Paul had graduated from law school, the school had given them T-shirts and mugs. The mugs were yellow with the school's purple branding on one side and their names and graduation year on the other.

"Kids are still sleeping," Paul whispered as he tiptoed back downstairs. "Lila slept right through it, but you missed Kyle. He was all, 'Wha? Wha?' I told him to go back to bed, buddy, and he goes, 'Okay,' and face-plants on the pillow." Paul snickered, then said, "Wow, that cup sent a broken piece all the way over here."

He knelt at the foot of the stairs and picked up the piece. "It's the handle."

"What?"

"The handle." He held it out to Karen.

Karen stared at the curved yellow C-shaped piece held between Paul's fingers—then looked down at the collection of pieces she'd gathered in her hand. She picked out a choice piece and held it up next to Paul's.

She, too, had a yellow handle.

"What the hell," Paul said, sounding more irritated than shocked, "Did mine break, too? I thought I—"

"Put it over there?" Karen finished for him as she pointed to where his mug still sat on the armrest tray of his side of the chair. "Nope, yours did not break. Yours is perfectly still intact."

"Then... how the hell...?"

There was the sentiment Karen had been expecting: How the hell, indeed?

"We only have two of these?" Paul said, stating the obvious. "The only other mugs we have are those Christmas mugs from my mom."

"I know," Karen said.

"So how the hell...?"

He took her handle piece and held it side by side with his own. Their matching yellow curves faced one way, and their ragged and exposed white edges faced the other.

"There's two friggin' handles here?" Paul said, "How the hell are there two friggin' handles?"

Karen sat back on her heels, feeling warm and validated.

"That, my friend, is a glitch."

And they didn't need video confirmation for this one. The proof was in Paul's hand.

"We're not throwing these away," he said, taking the two broken handle pieces to the kitchen.

Karen stood and followed after him, the mug's other big pieces still held in her hand.

Paul pulled a sandwich-sized plastic bag from the drawer to the right of the stove and stuffed the two handle pieces inside. He sealed it tightly, running his thumb and finger over the closure mechanism several times, then setting it on the counter. He grabbed another bag from the drawer—this one thicker and quart-sized—and held it open for Karen.

"Here," he said. "Put the pieces in here for now. I'm gonna see if I can put it back together."

"The handles, too?" Karen asked innocently.

"Which one, right?" He grinned at her. It was one of those cocky and yet disbelieving grins that can only happen when you're still in the middle of the magic moment. And a shared moment at that. It was the kind of grin that could never form on your face if you were experiencing the moment alone. You had to be with someone else, grinning at someone else, someone who was there and witnessing the same thing as you, understanding it like you.

And Karen knew she was giving Paul the exact same grin in return.

But moments are fleeting.

"Here," she said, dumping the big chunks of mug into Paul's bag. "I gotta clean up the mess before the kids get up."

She ripped a line of paper towels off the roll stuck to the wall and headed back to the chair, dropping the paper towels on the floor at the first drop of coffee she saw. Paul was right; the mess had traveled all the way to the kitchen doorway, where the hardwood turned into tile. She pulled her socks off and stepped onto the wad of paper towels, then nudged the wad around the hardwood floor with her feet as she made her way back to the mess by the chair, the scene of the glitch.

She didn't find any more noteworthy mug pieces or coffee splatters. When she was done cleaning up, she stuffed all the used paper towels into the garbage. It was full now, so she pulled out the bag, cinched it closed, and tied the red handles together, then set it on the floor and put a new bag into the bin.

"I'm just gonna take this out," she said to Paul, picking up the bulging garbage bag again and holding it out for him to see.

He'd put his plastic bags of broken pieces into a bowl on the counter and was now whipping up breakfast. Eggs, it looked like. Or maybe French toast. The pan was on the stove and the overhead vent was roaring.

"Okay," he said.

She headed downstairs to the garage, but the bin was not in its usual spot against the wall just inside the left garage bay door. She unlatched the lock on the garage door and lifted it up overhead.

Ah. There the gray container was. It was still sitting next to the big blue recycling container out on the sidewalk. Garbage day had been Friday morning and theirs was the only pair still left on the street. *Sorry, neighbors.*

She opened the garbage can's lid, stuffed the bag inside, and dragged it back to the house, then went back for the recycling container.

Sunrise was still a while off, but under the streetlights, she saw a man walking down the sidewalk on the other side of the street.

He had a very forward-leaning stride. His hands were stuffed into the pockets of his jeans.

He had on a yellow trucker hat, the kind with meshing at the back, and he wore one of those red-and-black plaid insulated hunting jackets.

He seemed to be in a hurry, definitely headed somewhere else. But he was watching her. And not just with his eyes. His whole head was turned in her direction.

He gave her an odd feeling. She waved at him, hoping to ease it.

The man nodded once, slowly dipping his chin to his shoulder, but his gaze did not waver, and neither did his expression, a kind of uber-intense focus.

Karen took note of him—of his dark hair and his six-foot height and his slender build—just in case.

Chapter 11

$\mathbf{B}$e unexpected.

Interfere with the pattern.

The universe behaves differently when someone is looking.

Paul was on board now. And after they'd shown them the broken cup and the two handles at the breakfast table, so were the kids.

"I want to make something glitch!"

"Yeah, I want to make something glitch!"

"You don't *make* something glitch," Karen heard herself tell them—even though she felt the opposite. She felt like the mug had broken the way it had *for her*, in response to her. How could it not have? She'd been spending the past few days thinking about glitches and trying to make one happen, and nothing like this, not quite like this, had ever happened to her before.

And yet something she defaulted to calling her 'protective instincts' was roaring through her lips and dampening everyone's excitement. She didn't want Lila and Kyle doing anything stupid or dangerous in the name of making things glitch. "Strange things just sometimes happen," she said.

"When you're good," Paul added.

Karen glanced at him. The same thought had popped into her mind, too, but she'd chosen not to say it out loud. It had felt too manipulative. Her kids were already pretty good.

Paul was grinning, like he'd only meant it as a joke.

But Lila and Kyle both sat up straighter, already trying to be even more good.

Already assimilating the programming.

Karen's own thought made her wince, and she wondered if she was going to come to regret her introduction to the idea, the metaphor, that the world behaved like a computer simulation, a video game, with people being nothing more than blank-slate characters that required programming. Something about the way Lila and Kyle—too young to understand that he was joking—had just accepted what Paul had said as truth, as the way things were, made her heart feel sick.

But she didn't know how to undo it, what to say to them about it.

And then the moment to say anything passed.

Chapter 12

"I found three of the same flowers!" Kyle said as he ran up to Karen after school that day, holding a fistful of dandelions. "Is this a glitch?"

Karen was standing on the sidewalk corner of the school's property with Molly and the tut-tutters.

"A what?" one of them tutted to the others. "What did he say?"

"A glitch," Molly told them, and then she waved it all away. "Never mind."

"I told you that's not a glitch," Lila said, plodding up behind Kyle.

But Kyle wasn't having it from Lila. "Is it a glitch, Mom?"

Karen, Paul, and the kids had spent their early breakfast talking about glitches and what constituted a glitch. Karen had shared the ones she'd remembered: the Mandela Effect and deja vu and identical copy-and-paste stranger sightings, and objects disappearing and reappearing in weird places.

"One time," she told the kids, "your dad found a little silver medallion out on the sidewalk." She turned to Paul. "Do you remember that? It was right after Kyle was born."

"Yeah," Paul said, blanching to the same pale expression he'd had when he'd first shown her the medallion all those years ago.

"What happened?" Lila asked.

"It had your grandparents' names on the back. My parents," she clarified. "I've still got it. Do you want to see?"

Kyle and Lila nodded eagerly.

Karen hadn't thought of the medallion as a glitch at the time Paul had shown it to her; she'd thought it was weird, but that was all. But it had been a glitch. It had been. And here she'd just put it on her desk and thought nothing more of it.

Until now.

She wondered what other things or occurrences in her life she had overlooked as insignificant.

She went upstairs to the little desk that was tucked away in a corner of the tiny spare bedroom that was mostly used for Paul's office. Sometimes when she was home alone with spare time on her hands, she fancied herself an aspiring blogger or maybe even an influencer. Never mind that she still hadn't settled on a topic to talk about. Still, she had some fun little inspirational tchotchkes set up on her computer stand that she sometimes played with to get herself into the mood. She grabbed the little St. Christopher medallion off the glass monitor stand and went back downstairs.

She set the medallion face down on the table in front of the kids and pointed at the engraving on the back.

CURT + MARIE

ICH LIEBE DICH

"What does *that* say?" Lila asked, pointing at the second line.

"*Ich liebe dich,*" Karen said, pretty sure she was pronouncing it atrociously. "It means 'I love you' in German. And you want to know the craziest part?"

Lila and Kyle nodded, their eyes wide.

"I called your grandma and told her we found a medallion with her and Dad's names on it, and that it said something weird under that, and she said '*Ich liebe dich?*'"

Karen could still hear the way her mom's tone had risen with the question. Her dad had died a couple years earlier, and her mom's voice had held so much emotion: astonishment, excitement, nostalgia.

"You never told me that," Paul said.

It was technically true. She hadn't told him that she'd called her mom about the medallion because he'd been in the same room with her when Karen had been on the phone. He had a tendency to tune her out when she was talking to her mom. His bad.

"Yeah," she said to him, and she returned her attention to the kids. "She said your grandpa bought it for her when they were dating."

"Whoa," Kyle said.

"Yeah," Karen said. "It's pretty old. And you want to know the really craziest part?"

They nodded.

"Your grandma had already moved to Florida by then. She hadn't been to the house in years. So how was it suddenly out on the sidewalk?"

Lila and Kyle had looked at each other with appreciative, wide-eyed gravitas.

And Paul had said, "I'd say that's a glitch."

And from there on out, the kids had been all about finding their own glitches.

Lila had remembered how she'd discovered three dimes in one day, and Karen had told her that the dimes could very well count as a glitch, the dime on the desk especially, but maybe even all three together as a triple sighting.

This had left Kyle determined to find his own triple sighting. Just that morning, after Paul had left for work but before it was time to leave for school, he'd shown Karen three white rocks that he'd found in the gravel alongside the fence; three sets of building bricks, where a skinny white brick was stuck on top of a regular-sized red brick; and three different-sized snails sliming up and down Paul's tomato plants.

And now he was shaking his fistful of three sad dandelions up at Karen. "Is it, Mom? Is it a glitch?"

"I've created monsters," Karen whispered to Molly as she tried to nudge her two kids toward the car and put some space between them and the tut-tutters.

"At least they're cute monsters," Molly said. She collected her son, Cole, and waved bye as they wandered away.

"Is it, Mom?" Kyle said. "Is it a glitch?"

Karen knelt down in front of him. "I don't know, buddy. How'd you find them?"

"He just picked them off the playground," Lila said.

"Is that true?" Karen asked, and it struck her that the way she was talking to him both felt and sounded like she was chastising him for lying. That wasn't what she intended. Glitches should be fun, not whatever that accusatory voice was trying to make them out to be. She tried to perk up her tone. "How did you select them?"

"They were just the first three he came to," Lila said. "I saw him. He just picked the first three."

Kyle's pink bottom lip poked out and then started curving down.

"Hey," Karen said, taking him by the upper arms and looking into his eyes. "They're good flowers, okay? No matter how you picked them, why you picked them, or whether or not they're a glitch. Okay?"

"They're not a glitch," he said, burying his wet face into her shoulder.

Karen hugged him and smiled sympathetically at Lila. This wasn't Lila's fault. Lila wasn't wrong about the flowers; Karen didn't think they were a glitch, either. And Karen understood the inclination to point out to people what was true and what wasn't. Although, that inclination had lessened a lot since having kids—especially Kyle—and experiencing moments like these.

Lila put a comforting hand on Kyle's shoulder.

Kyle sniffled and Karen pulled back. "Shall we head to the car?"

Kyle wiped his eyes and nodded.

His dandelions had fallen to the sidewalk.

"Do you want to take your flowers?" Karen asked.

Without looking at the dandelions, Kyle slipped his hand into hers and shook his head as he started leading them toward where she usually parked the car, away from the discarded would-be glitch.

Chapter 13

Kyle may not have been finding glitches, but Karen felt like she was seeing triple sightings everywhere. Three red cars in a row idling next to her at a red light. Three of the same numbers in a row every time she looked at a clock. Three strangers in close proximity all wearing the same colored jacket or the same team's jersey.

"Those aren't glitches," Molly had told her when they'd been waiting for the kids on the sidewalk corner before the dandelion incident. Karen had already told her about the two broken mug handles. Molly had been thoroughly impressed. "That's synchronicity," she said. "That's the universe confirming that you're in alignment."

"In alignment with what?"

"In alignment with yourself."

Karen had seen Kyle and Lila right after that, so there hadn't been time to ask Molly anything more. But Karen thought it was pretty cool how the universe was using what was around her to talk to her in its own way. And she was starting to get a better feel for how that communication worked. So elegant. So personalized.

But what did it mean to be in alignment with herself? There

was just one of her. So how could she ever *not* be in alignment with herself?

She pondered this idea as she drove the kids home, this idea of alignment and of being aligned with herself.

It struck her that, although she was just one person, if she counted who she'd been in the past, then that was another person, another point with which to make a line. And if she counted who she would be in the future, then that was another person, another point that may or may not be in alignment with the other two. Was that what Molly had meant?

Maybe. But it didn't really resonate with Karen. The past was done. Whether it had been in alignment or not, there was nothing she could do about it now.

But what about Future Karen?

Present Karen felt the question resonate as soon as she verbalized it in her mind; she felt her body grow warm and full. So what might alignment have to do with Future Karen? Present Karen supposed that depending on her choices now, Future Karen was—

"Mom?"

"Yeah," Karen said, glancing in the rearview mirror at Lila.

Seated behind Karen, Lila was leaning into the center of the back seat, trying to be seen. But then she made a confused face and sat back in her seat, disappearing again.

"Nothing," she said.

"You sure?"

"Uh-huh."

"You can tell me anything, you know."

"I know."

Karen waited for Lila to say something, but she didn't.

"Okay," Karen said, and she focused on the road.

But she felt herself frowning. She had a nagging feeling that she was forgetting something. That Lila had distracted her from something she'd been thinking about, some insight she'd been on the verge of having about something. But she couldn't remember what it was.

Be unexpected.

Interfere with the pattern.

The universe behaves differently when someone is looking.

Lila had ballet on Mondays.

The class was two hours long, but the school was housed in a building that was part of a huge community complex with shops, a theater, a gym, and both indoor and outdoor parks, so usually the whole family went.

The complex had a daycare where Karen and Paul left Kyle if they couldn't help it, but usually they each took him for an hour while the other went to the gym or got a hair cut.

Today, though, they both took him to the bank.

They had less than half an hour before it closed for the day, and they stood third in line. As they waited, Karen thought about being in line, about being in alignment, and about how those two phrases really didn't mean the same thing.

Getting in line meant joining the queue, sure, but it also had a ring of conformity—of getting in line with what everyone else was doing, of order imposed from the outside.

Alignment was about being in line, too, but it was more about—

"Hey, Karen?"

"Yeah?"

She shook her focus clear and turned toward Paul, but he wasn't standing next to her anymore. He and Kyle were standing in front of one of the little square openings in the glass partition that ran along the teller counter.

"Oh," she said, joining them.

Alignment, she told herself, trying to save the thought for later as she turned her attention to the bank teller. She'd been thinking about alignment.

After leaving the bank, Karen let Kyle drag her everywhere he wanted to go—the toy store, the pet store, the electronics store, the playground—while Paul went to play a pick-up game of basketball on the outdoor court with a ragtag group of older kids and adults, the likes of which he often sat across the aisle from at work, in a different kind of court. Karen and Paul had agreed to meet back at ballet on the hour. But with fifteen minutes to go, Paul called and asked her to meet him early.

"There's Dad," Kyle said, pointing across the courtyard.

Paul trudged up to them in his long basketball shorts. He usually carried his gym bag over one shoulder, but he had it slung across his chest and hanging behind him.

He was gripping one wrist to keep the hand steady. His fingers looked like sausages.

"What happened?" Karen asked.

"Guy passed me the ball when I wasn't expecting it, and I jammed my hand."

"Is it broken? Do you need to go see the doctor?"

"Nah. They move." Paul's fingers slowly clenched halfway

into a fist and then relaxed again. "It doesn't hurt, really," he said, even though he was wincing. "It's just stiff. I'll ice it when we get home. Can you drive?"

They'd driven Paul's car, another SUV even older than Karen's. Karen fiddled with the seat adjustments, moving it forward and up. Then she adjusted the side mirrors so that she could see her blind spots.

"Never mind, I'll drive," Paul said with a laugh.

She grinned at him. "Jerk."

She grabbed the rearview mirror and adjusted it until she could see out the back—and what she saw made her suck in a breath.

"Everything okay?" Paul asked.

She checked the mirror again. Just beyond the two rows of mostly empty parking stalls behind her was the main public road, and the guy she'd seen on the sidewalk was still there. And he was still wearing what she'd thought he was wearing: a red-and-black plaid thermal hunting jacket. He even had on a yellow trucker's hat; the yellow mesh was riding high on the back of his head.

But he was too heavy to be the guy she'd seen the morning she'd taken out the trash after breaking her law school mug.

And anyway, he wasn't looking at her. He was just minding his own business, and now he was getting onto a bus.

"Yup," Karen said. "All good."

But she put her hands at ten and two on the wheel in front of her and closed her eyes, steadying herself, just for a minute, before turning on the car.

Big, wet raindrops started drenching the windshield.

It was probably about time it rained for real, if Karen was being honest. They'd had an amazing summer, and it had persisted well into the fall. It was almost Halloween. Their neighbors had long ago put up decorations. Karen still hadn't decided if she and Paul were bad parents for deciding to wait until the kids asked about putting up store-bought decorations before finally (if ever, fingers crossed) getting around to doing it. Paul, the big kid, always eventually got the urge to carve a pumpkin, and so far he'd been able to satisfy any desires the kids had to decorate these past few years by entertaining them with the activity. He would get them each a big, proper pumpkin from the store and then carve up whatever squash he'd managed to grow in the yard. His designs were pretty good, too. Just as good and sometimes even better than those fake carved pumpkins she saw in people's yards. Karen was always plenty satisfied with their own festiveness. And after Halloween, the spent pumpkins went into the compost instead of into the garage. She dreaded the day when they might have to invest in—and then store—a two-story skeleton or a collection of inflatables.

Karen turned on her windshield wipers and then backed out of her parking spot.

When she looked back out her front windshield again, she saw a fat raindrop slide down the glass. It stopped suddenly, in perfect horizontal alignment with two other fat drops, before all three were wiped away.

"Huh," Karen uttered.

"Did you say something?" Paul asked.

"What? No. Just thinking."

She made her way down the feeder lane and came up on a car

with its brake lights on. Karen leaned to the left to see what the holdup was. Another driver was having a hell of a time trying to back a huge Suburban into a parking space.

Karen was in line behind two other cars.

That's right. She'd been thinking about alignment earlier, when they'd been standing in line at the bank. She'd been thinking about how *being in line* and *being in alignment* sounded like the same thing but actually kinda weren't. The two phrases had different connotations. But not the kind of connotation you felt right away, the kind that hit you in the gut emotionally as soon as the words were said. Instead, they had the kind of subtle connotation you only noticed after thinking about the words for a bit, the kind that, in this case, was slowly making Karen feel cheated.

The Suburban got itself squared away and the traffic started moving. Karen inched forward, trying to hold on to her thoughts about alignment. She pulled out of the parking lot and got herself settled in the right-hand lane, heading east on Andresen. Her turnoff was miles ahead.

On first hearing, the phrases *being in line* and *being in alignment* both sounded like good things. If you were 'in line,' then you would eventually get served, you would get what you needed.

But Karen could think of all sorts of times when she'd stood in line only to reach the end and be turned away for whatever reason. Just recently, she'd stood in line at the DMV, trying to get the new ID card everyone said she needed, and the clerk had turned her away because she didn't have the right paperwork. Paul had held the same paperwork she'd had, and he'd gotten his ID just fine. But Karen had been told that since the married name on her driver's license didn't match the maiden name on her birth certificate, she had to come back with a certified marriage certificate and stand in line again. She'd been so annoyed about it that she still hadn't gotten around to doing it. And the more she'd thought about it at the time, the more the whole thing had just sounded pointless. Why a new ID? How was it at all necessary? She'd eventually let it all go because she had a passport, which could serve the same duty as the ID, and so complying with the new rule hadn't really affected her.

But thinking about it all again now, about how she'd stood in line... and for what? For nothing. And it still would have been for nothing even if she had gotten a new ID. It had all felt needless at the time—not just the wait and being turned away, but the request that she do any of it at all—but now something about it made it feel not only pointless but violative.

And she knew what that something was, how standing in that line, in any line, how *being in line* differed from being in alignment.

Nobody got in line because they wanted to; they did it because they were told. Being in line was order imposed. It was someone else's order being imposed upon her, upon people. Whereas being in alignment—

"Karen, look out!"

Karen's eyes flashed alert on the bright green traffic light up ahead and the dark, wet road in front of her.

Someone in a red-and-black plaid jacket and a yellow trucker hat strode into the crosswalk. Karen slammed on her brakes—but the SUV slid forward.

The man in the crosswalk turned to face her.

Karen veered right, swerving around him, and the SUV jumped the curb—thump, thump.

The car came to a stop.

Karen's heart was pounding and her skin was sweating.

Beside her, Paul put a hand on her arm as he turned to look into the back seat.

"You all right? Everyone all right?"

Karen didn't hear anything else that was said. Instead, she heard a ringing in her ears, a loud piercing noise. But then it faded away, taking her disorientation with it.

She looked out her side window at the crosswalk.

The man was gone. Like he had never been there at all. The traffic was flowing under the still-green light.

"You saw that, didn't you?" Karen said. "The guy in the street?"

"*Yeah,* I saw him," Paul said. "I saw him watching the cars. I thought he was just timing them for a gap to dash across the street, but then he stepped right out in front of you."

Right out in front of you.

Paul hadn't emphasized the word, but Karen heard it that way anyway.

"Do you see him now?" she asked.

Paul put his good hand on the dash and leaned this way and that, still strapped into his seat belt.

"You don't see him, do you?" Karen asked.

"No. Where'd he go?"

"Where'd who go?" Lila asked.

"A guy in a red-and-black jacket," Paul said, and Karen's whole body alighted with tingles. Paul had seen him, too. He'd really seen him. "And a yellow hat. Do you see anyone like that?"

The kids looked around, but they didn't see him.

"Where'd he go?" Paul asked.

"Was he a glitch?" Kyle asked, clearly eager for the situation to be classified as such. His first experienced glitch.

Karen couldn't lie to him; she couldn't tell him that it wasn't.

Paul was looking at her like he had the same question, but she didn't know what to say to him, either.

So she said nothing as she eased the SUV between a thankfully empty bus shelter, on the right, and a light pole she had just barely missed hitting, on the left. The car thump-thumped off the sidewalk as she angled it onto the road that headed south. She then flipped a U-ey around a median curb and headed back to the intersection so that she could turn back onto Andresen and continue east toward their house.

The SUV worked fine. All that excitement could have ended so much worse, and yet they were going home in one piece.

Thank you.

Alignment.

The word popped into her mind unbidden, almost like a response. And she welcomed the reminder.

She kept a better eye on the road this time, but she resumed her thoughts about alignment as she drove her family home.

And the concepts were a lot clearer now.

Almost like the ringing in your ears had been a download.

Karen winced at the thought, at the computer-simulation metaphor making sense once again. But she couldn't say it was wrong.

Being in line was following an order, an order imposed upon her from the outside.

But being in alignment was different.

It was order achieved from the inside.

If her alignment matched up with what was wanted on the

outside, that was great, that was fine—because it was order achieved by her own informed agreement.

But being in compliance with the outside world was incidental; it was secondary, if it mattered at all. What mattered was being in alignment.

Chapter 14

The next morning, Karen took the kids to school early and then hung around at the corner, hoping to catch Molly.

She supposed she could have called her; she had Molly's phone number. But Molly was a working single mom, and Karen didn't want to bug her. She might be busy.

Or at least, that's what Karen had told herself. Truth was, she didn't want to talk about any of this over the phone where her kids might be listening. Paul, too, for that matter. No, she wanted to talk about this in close confidence and with hushed voices. She wanted the wind roaring by so that no one else could hear.

Karen was checking her watch, expecting the bell to ring anytime soon, when she saw Karen's two-toned Camry. The silver and red car pulled up alongside the curb on the front-facing side of the school just long enough for Cole to hop out and race for the front door.

Karen ran down the sidewalk waving her arms.

"Molly!"

The Camry was about to speed off past the yellow twenty-miles-per-hour school-zone lights—which were still flashing despite the fact that Karen was the only person on the street—when the car suddenly slammed to a stop.

Molly reached across the front passenger seat and rolled down the window as Karen ran up to meet her.

"I'm late for work," Molly said.

"Okay," Karen said, but she bent down to talk to Molly through the window anyway. "I need to talk to John again."

"Okay, I'll call him and get back to you. Good?"

"Yeah. Thank you."

Molly waved and sped off without rolling the window back up.

Karen hoofed it back to her car. The sky was a blanket of dark gray clouds, and the air had a wet chill. Only a smattering of fall leaves remained on the trees. Karen aligned the bottoms of the zipper on the hoodie she was wearing and zipped it up to her chin.

Karen went to the store to pick up some potatoes to bake for dinner that night, and then she headed home.

The left-turn light into her neighborhood changed to red as she approached. She stopped at the white line and rested her foot on the brake, her elbow on the side panel, and settled in for the wait.

This was always a long light. As usual, the oncoming lanes were empty of traffic. She could see nothing but smooth pavement for at least five blocks, where another light was holding back other drivers.

There was no traffic on the side streets, either. There rarely was.

She looked around. On her left was a hospital with

manicured green lawns. The rest of the buildings near the intersection were all small houses, some of them still residential, some of them converted into small shops.

But there were no pedestrians out. At least, none that Karen could see.

And the light was still red.

Should she do it?

Her heart pounded at just the idea of it, the idea of transgression, minor though it would be. It wasn't like she'd be hurting anyone. There was literally no one around. So why all the hesitation, all the fear of getting caught? Why was every cell in her body telling her to not do it when she was the only person here being inconvenienced by an arbitrary, poorly timed light? It was a *light*, for goodness' sake. A light. A light she felt forced to obey, every day, day after day. It wasn't even a living, breathing—

Her foot moved off the brake and slammed on the gas, and she pulled into the intersection. The shock of her actions rose from her chest in a sustained cry as she leaned hard on the wheel to make the turn. The tires screeched around the corner—

And she was through!

The steering wheel turned back to neutral and the car straightened out.

She took her foot off the gas, hoping the slowing car would slow the panic in her chest.

Karen listened for police sirens, but heard none, not even the sirens of ambulances headed to the hospital.

A woman walking her dog further down the street was looking back at the intersection, making a face like she wasn't sure what all that tire screeching had been about. But she must've decided it was nothing, because she turned back around and kept walking, her little dog sniffing the grass along the way.

It was nothing.

So why did it feel like something?

Not just something she'd done, but something more.

Something she'd become.

Be unexpected.

Interfere with the pattern.

The universe behaves differently when no one is looking.

Well, apparently, so did Karen.

And that left turn of hers on a red arrow had definitely been unexpected. Her pattern had always been to wait for the whims of the light, any light. Any order. She'd always been a good kid. She'd always been one who obeyed.

And the realization made her angry.

Chapter 15

At lunchtime, Molly called. Karen told Molly about the guy in the plaid jacket jumping out in front of their car, and Molly told Karen that John was in town running errands today and that he could meet her at the Mills Park Library.

He was easy to spot. And not just because he was a big bearded guy chatting it up with the clerks at the checkout desk just inside the entrance doors. Karen had immediately honed in on what he was wearing, and it stopped her in her tracks.

"Can I help you?" said one of the clerks John was talking to.

John looked over his shoulder at her. "Karen? You okay? You look like you saw a ghost."

She looked from the red-and-black plaid thermal hunting jacket he was wearing up to his concerned bearded face.

"No," she said. "It's just that you're wearing what I came to talk to you about."

John's lips slowly curved upward into a smile, like things were going even better than he'd expected.

Karen didn't know what *she* had expected, but it wasn't a smile like that.

John turned to his clerk friends. "Can we get one of the rooms?" he said. "The one in the back corner. Is that available?"

It was, until the top of the hour, anyway. John led her back there, through the study tables and then the stacks.

The room had a square window that looked in on its bare white walls and round Formica table and four gray chairs, but it was otherwise private. Quiet, at any rate. John held the door open for her.

She took the seat that put her back to the window. She wasn't worried about being snuck up on at the library. She was, however, worried about being seen. Not seen with John; but seen saying what she was about to say with all the expression it would undoubtedly plaster all over her face.

Instead of sitting across from her, John sat to her left. He turned toward her, resting one forearm on the table, the other on the back of his chair. He was giving her more than just his full attention. He was giving her a safe space.

Karen eyed his red-and-black thermal jacket.

John looked down at it. "Do you want me to take it off?"

Karen shook her head. She figured she'd like it even less resting on the table with nobody in it.

"So I've seen some more glitches," she said.

"Let's hear it."

"I broke my mug the other day, and when I picked up the pieces, there were two handles."

"Yup," John said with a nod.

"You've seen that before?"

"Sure. Duplicate pieces. Pieces that look like they should fit, but they're curved the wrong way, but then when they're placed with the curve facing the right direction, they no longer fit."

"Really?" Karen said about that last one. "That's so weird.

I've seen some triple sightings, too, but Molly said those were synchronicities."

"Telling you that you're on the right path," John said, nodding. "That's good."

"On the right path," Karen said with a snort, and then her gaze moved to John's red-and-black plaid jacket again. She could feel herself glaring at it. "It doesn't *feel* like I'm on the right path."

John pulled at the fabric. "Something to do with the jacket?"

Karen nodded. "So after the mug thing, finding the two handles, I took the garbage out and I saw this guy walking down the street looking at me funny, just staring. A dead-eyed stare. He was wearing a jacket like yours and a yellow hat. You know the trucker hats with the foam front and the mesh back? It was like that."

"And then later you saw him again," John said.

"Yeah," Karen said, not bothering to ask John how he knew that. "Not him, though. It was another guy, a bigger guy. But he had on the same jacket, like yours, and also the same yellow hat."

"And?" John said. "Did something happen?"

"I was in the car with Paul and the kids. I guess I wasn't paying attention. I'd been thinking about something—"

"You got distracted?"

"What?" Karen said.

But she'd heard him. And she started recalling all the things she'd been doing over the past few days that, in some way, big or small, had gotten interrupted: the documentary about glitches she'd been watching with Paul when she'd gotten the call to pick up Kyle; the thing she'd been thinking about in the car but then forgot when Lila said her name for no reason. But also the interruption that happened when Paul got her attention at the bank, and the way her internet searches got interrupted by the computer giving her an error message.

John must've realized she was doing some serious thinking, because he didn't interrupt—he didn't distract her. He let her follow the line of thought to a conclusion.

"The guy in the jacket," she said. "I'd been thinking about alignment, about how 'being in line' sounds a lot like 'being in alignment,' but how it's not the same at all, not *at all*," she said, feeling the anger again at her expanding realizations. "I'd been thinking about how the world had duped me into thinking they were the same, and at that moment, the guy stepped into the road—to distract me? How could that be? How could he know what I was thinking about? And why would he care even if he did?"

Karen looked up at John and found that he was smiling.

"Congratulations," he said. "You have touched the boundary."

Karen shook her head. "What boundary?"

"The boundary between this physical world and everything it's hiding. The boundary between running the default programming in complacent ignorance, and writing your own."

Karen snorted at John's use of the computer metaphor, and he stopped talking, even though Karen got the sense he could've kept going.

But she didn't ask him to continue. What he'd said was already a lot to unpack. She sat with it a moment, and her lazy mind grabbed on to the easiest part to tease out.

"I was reading a little about simulation theory," she said,

"that we're all avatars in a computer game. Do you really believe that?"

"Literally? No. But I think it's the best metaphor we've got so far."

"How come not literally?"

John palmed his chest and looked off to the side at nothing, or maybe at everything.

"The idea of literally being in a computer simulation doesn't feel good," he said. "I've learned to go by what feels good. Not wild good. But calm good. And 'literally' doesn't feel good." He nodded as if satisfied with his answer, and then he dropped his hand from his chest and smiled at her.

"I like that logic," Karen said.

"I think some people would take offense at you calling it 'logic,' but I have to say I agree, and I like it, too. It's led me true so far."

Karen felt herself sigh, and for the first time since last night on the drive home from the community complex, she could feel that her whole body had finally relaxed.

"How did you know I got distracted?" she asked.

"It's the way it works. Far as I can tell, anyway. You touch the boundary when you refuse to be distracted away from it, away from the ideas that things are different from what we're taught, that there's more to this world than what we're told. The distractions seem like random coincidence, but I don't think they are. I think of them as forces. We think it's only other people enforcing the narrative programming—and they are; don't get me wrong—but it doesn't *feel* like it's just physical people maintaining the status quo. It feels like it's something else, too, something more."

John put his hand to his chest again, and Karen found

herself doing the same. She closed her eyes and focused in on her chest, on the sensations behind her sternum, just beyond her palm. Her inner chest felt clenched up like a fist.

"I don't want to get all conspiracy theory or whatever," Karen said, "but the past few days—I do feel like I've been shoved around a bit."

"By forces?"

She nodded.

"Did all of them feel bad?"

"No, not all of them, I guess. The synchronicities felt good. Fun. And the mug was fun. Actually, the mug was incredible."

"That's good," John said. "It's good you can already tell the difference."

"Between what?"

"Between the forces."

Karen grimaced. "I'm getting the feeling you're telling me they're not going to stop."

"Ha!" John laughed. "Sorry, kid."

"Great," she said, simultaneously dreading the bad ones while eagerly anticipating the good ones. "So what do I do now?"

Chapter 16

"He said that when you push against the boundary, the forces that don't want you to cross it will start pushing back," Karen said.

She was telling Paul about her meeting with John. They'd left Kyle under the floodlights at the T-ball practice field and were taking a walk around Treeline Park, where they couldn't be overheard. The skies were cloudy, but the air still smelled crisp. The coming rainfall was probably another couple hours off. Through the cedar trees, Karen could see Lila hop off a swing and run to the merry-go-round, where some of the other T-ball siblings were pushing it to go faster.

"He said the boundary is between complacent ignorance, on the one side, and not only noticing the glitches but sincerely asking what they mean and acting on that knowledge, on the other."

"Did he say what they mean?" Paul asked. "The glitches?"

"No. He said he has his own ideas about what they are and what they mean but that there was no point in sharing them with me. He said the goal wasn't knowledge through being told what's true—he says that's the basis of the world's whole problem in the first place. He said the goal is to know through experience."

"Through experience," Paul said. "Like school of hard knocks, that kind of thing?"

"I don't know. Maybe," Karen said. But the more she considered it, the more that didn't sound right. "Actually, I don't think so. I think hard knocks happen—well, actually, I'm not sure why they happen. But I'm thinking they don't need to happen. He—John—he kept putting his hand to his chest, like he could feel the—I don't know—the knowing, I guess. Like the knowing was here."

Karen patted her chest.

"And that made sense to me," she said. "Like, you can feel what's right, and you can feel what's off, even if you're being told it's right. You can feel what's just plain wrong. You know?"

"I do," he said. "It's like when the law tells me to treat someone brought in on a charge one way, and something in me—I just can't do it. I do everything I can to plea them down to something less. Sometimes a lot less. Community service."

Karen looked up at him, struck by his humanity, and hugged him from the side, burying her face into his shoulder. He'd never told her that before.

"I love you," she said, looking up at him again. "I love that about you."

He pulled his arm out of her hug and wrapped it around her, kissing the top of her head. "Love you, too. So what did he tell you to do?"

"John? He said to keep an eye out and to pay attention to when I'm getting distracted, because chances are if I'm being distracted, it means my train of thought is on the right track."

"The right track?"

"To break through the boundary. He told me the first time I met him that the glitches were just the beginning. Their main purpose is to get my attention. 'There's something over here, Karen. Do you want to come see?' That kind of thing. And by leaning into it, by thinking about them, I said yes. I leaned into the boundary."

"I still don't get the boundary," Paul said. "What boundary?"

"I don't really get it either," Karen said. "But John said to not think about it as a thing or a place. He said to not even think about it as a fact. He said he wasn't telling me facts, he was telling me truths. And that I got; there's a difference between fact and truth. He was telling me how it feels to bump up against the boundary, because my eyes weren't going to see it. At best, they were just going to see the people and things the forces use to protect it."

"Like the guy in the red-and-black jacket?"

"Don't forget the yellow hat." Karen said with a derisive snort. "You know John was wearing that kind of jacket today? Not the hat, just the jacket, the red-and-black plaid. I thought it was the oddest, creepiest thing, and he was like, 'Really? You've got one foot across the boundary. I don't think this moment could've happened any other way.' He told me he wasn't planning on wearing a jacket at all, because he runs hot and wasn't expecting to be outside, but then he just grabbed it off the rack on the way out to his truck."

"For you," Paul said.

"You know, I asked him that. He said, 'Of course for you. Who else would I have grabbed it for?' He said he doesn't even like the jacket because the fit's too small. It's all just so crazy."

They walked on in silence for a few steps. Karen checked the playground for Lila and then the field for Kyle. Both kids were still accounted for.

"So which forces do you think made him grab the jacket?" Paul asked.

"Which forces?"

"The good forces or the bad forces?"

Karen blew out a breath, wubbling her lips. "I don't know. Seeing him in it scared the shit outa me for a second, I'm not gonna lie. But then..." She shrugged. "I don't know. It all turned out okay, I guess, in the end."

Chapter 17

Karen and Paul hadn't even gotten the kids rounded up and back into the car after T-ball practice when Karen began to understand why John had used the words *complacent* ignorance.

Every time she started to think about something that might lead her deeper into the boundary, she found herself telling herself to think about it later.

Paul was driving and the kids were entertained in the back seat. She was free to stare out the dark window and let her mind wander, to let it wonder about things like alignment and what was on the other side of the boundary and what it might mean to her life if she crossed it.

But, no, she told herself. She should probably stay focused on the road, just in case someone in a red-and-black plaid jacket decided to jump out in front of their car again. She could think about that other stuff later.

She saw herself doing it, making the decision. She saw herself choosing to not pursue the questions. She wondered if she could blame her hesitancy on the forces trying to distract her, trying to keep her from leaning in. And maybe she could blame them for her initial thought that there was something better she should be doing with her time than thinking. But she couldn't blame the forces for how she chose to respond to them once she felt their impact.

And she couldn't blame the programming, either, not when she could see both choices. The goal of society's programming was to prevent people from seeing that they had a choice; she understood that now. So the fact that she could see both choices meant she was beyond the programming. Oh, sure, the programming could still render one choice easier to make, a lot easier to make, but she was still responsible for making it.

Or for not making it, as was the case for her in this moment. She felt stuck in a loop, considering which option to choose: think or don't think. But that in itself was a choice, wasn't it? If she only ever *debated* whether she should think about what the glitches meant, then she would never get around to actually thinking about what the glitches meant.

She knew what she should do, what she mostly wanted to do, but she just couldn't get herself to do it.

John had said that as far as he could tell, the path across the boundary was less like walking a well-worn foot trail and more like rowing a dinghy through the system of locks in the Panama Canal.

She had just asked him why glitches happen to people.

"They're always happening," he'd said. "The real question is why some people start paying attention. But once they do, they enter that first lock, and just like the water rising and closing off the ocean behind them, the glitches start increasing and there's no turning back."

He said that as far as he could tell, there were two sets of forces: the ones trying to get you to pay attention and the ones trying to keep you from realizing the truth.

"They're not subtle about it," he said. "Well, that's not true. The forces trying to distract you are subtle about it; it doesn't help their cause for you to start noticing what they're doing. But the forces trying to get you to pay attention and the forces who step up when distraction isn't working anymore? They're not sneaky about what they're doing, and they're not trying to be. They want you to see them. They want you to know they see you."

"How come it only feels like the negative forces are doing that?" Karen had asked.

"Because they have the support of the programming. We're constantly told to be careful, to not take risks, to not look too closely—not everybody, mind, just the majority of us. When the forces scare you, they're just reinforcing what you've already been taught, what you already think you know."

"What started the programming?"

"I don't know. People who managed to put themselves in charge, I guess. Whether they did it themselves or with the help of the forces..." John shrugged.

"And—what?—it's all just maintained by the people in charge now?"

"Not just maintained," he said. "It's built up. Reinforced. Everything you see and hear is meant to keep you thinking the approved thoughts and acting in the approved way—and I don't mean adhering to a certain set of manners and dress code and that kind of thing. The approved thought and behavior is to be and cause upset, period. Because if you go through life like that, you'll never know the boundary is even there. You'll never be a threat to the system. It'll still mess with you for other reasons, but not because you're a threat."

"And the forces trying to wake you up have to buck all that?"

"And *you* have to buck all that," he'd said. "It's not enough to learn about the boundary and the forces and the programming and its goal. You have to know it enough to enact it." He'd leaned back in his chair. "How you behave is what you know. If you're still acting out the programming, you don't know anything."

As Karen now sat in the front passenger seat of the SUV, staring out the window, she thought about what she thought she knew and how she'd been taught it.

And her mind wandered to Kyle. His first week of kindergarten, he'd been sent home with an official reprimand for climbing up the slide. He hadn't wanted to play on any playground equipment since then.

Karen, herself, had once had her desk moved to the front of the class, right up against the blackboard, in second grade, because she was too often (once) a hub of conversation during 'quiet time.' In sixth grade, she'd gotten kicked out of dance class for suggesting to the school's new teacher (who didn't come back the following year) that there was a less clunky way to move into a step. Karen was mostly the quiet sort now, keeping most of her thoughts to herself, and occasionally poor Paul.

Everyone in the world had started out like that, as creative and energetic little geniuses who never stood a chance.

That night, as she pressed her head to her pillow, she told herself she had no more excuses. There was no going back. The locks in the metaphysical canal she was in could only move her forward. She knew about glitches. She couldn't un-experience the egg or the mug. The shower faucet reminded her that it used to be different every time she turned it on. And just that morning, she'd seen the flickers again.

"It might be nothing," she had said to John as they were leaving the library. "But sometimes when I come out of the bathroom in the morning and the light is just right, my room flickers."

"Right before sunrise?"

"Yeah."

"The illusion's already cracking for you. You're further along than I thought."

"What do you mean cracking?"

"We think this is all seamless." He ran his hand over the top of a low bookshelf, making a smooth sliding sound as they passed by on their way out of the library. "Hour to hour. Room to room. Space to space. No gaps."

"Part of the programming?" she'd asked.

"The original part," he'd said. "But that's still all it is. Programming. Literally. Like TV programming. Have you ever seen the film of an old movie reel?"

"The brown strips of images, frame by frame?"

"That's the stuff. The light projecting the image stays in one place, and if the frames of images pass by the light fast enough, what appears on the wall looks like non-stop motion."

"But it's not."

"Nope, and when the film slows down, you can see the flickers."

Karen nodded. "So what makes the world's film slow down?" she asked.

"I don't think it does," John said. "The rate of change is said to be Planck's constant, something incomprehensibly fast. Even at half that speed, a quarter, a hundredth, you're not going to see it. I think the flickers are just another glitch, probably some trick of the light that can only happen at twilight. But it's enough to get you thinking. To get you wondering what exists between the flashes."

"Somehow that just makes it even more awesome," Karen said.

"My advice?" John said as he'd pulled the keys to his truck from his pocket. "Don't tell anyone you see the flickers. They'll just tell you to get your head checked."

Noted, she thought now with a smile as she snuggled into her bed, although she'd probably eventually tell Paul.

She fell asleep thinking about the left turn she'd made against the red arrow, her brush with trouble that had turned out to be no trouble at all. She'd felt so uncomfortable doing it that she still wasn't sure she'd ever do it again. And yet, she knew transgressions like that weren't even the point. There was a four-way stop near her home, where many times the drivers traveling on the dominant road would look her right in the eye as they blazed through their stop sign out of turn. That wasn't the kind of boundary Karen was trying to cross. She wasn't trying to do away with courtesy and consideration. Just with arbitrary attempts at control. Especially the stupid kind.

John had been impressed that she could feel the difference between the forces of awareness and the forces of distraction. But maybe she wasn't as good at distinguishing them as he had made it sound. She wondered if the red-arrow incident had been nothing more than a distraction. Not a distraction from her line of thought, but a distraction to guide her thoughts to the places those forces preferred her to go.

The forces that supported the programming.

The forces that manufactured conflict.

The forces that wanted control.

Perhaps when they failed to keep someone from touching the boundary, the forces of distraction shifted their efforts into making that person into just another disgruntled boot on the necks of others. And why not? Karen had no doubt awareness of the boundary could go both ways, positive or negative. And with the support of society's programming constantly bombarding her, upsetting her, she knew which way would be all too easy to follow if she wasn't constantly vigilant.

So much for debate and hesitancy, then.

Bye-bye, complacency.

Chapter 18

The next morning, she woke up to the flickers.

She had always wondered if seeing the flickers had anything to do with coming out of the bright bathroom into the dimly lit bedroom, but now she had her answer.

The bathroom light had nothing to do with it.

The flickers didn't last long, but for several seconds, as Paul puttered around the room getting ready for work under the dim upward-facing light, she saw the room quickly darken and brighten over and over again.

"Do you see the room flickering?" she asked him.

"What?"

"The room is flickering."

He finished buttoning his shirt and then looked around the room. But the flickers had faded.

"Never mind," Karen said. "It's gone now."

Paul opened his sock drawer, grabbed a pair, and then came around the side of the bed and kissed Karen. "I've got a deposition this morning that I'm not ready for, so I'm heading in early. Do we have anything tonight?"

"What's today? Wednesday?"

"Pretty sure."

"I don't think so. T-ball's tomorrow."

"Good deal. I'll call you if it runs late."

Karen stayed snuggled in her warm bed, listening to Paul putter around downstairs. He left through the door to the garage, and then the garage bay door creaked open. Karen got out of bed and headed into the bathroom.

When she came out, she saw the flickers again. It was the first time she'd ever seen them twice in one day. She tried to look extra carefully at the darker moments, the gaps between the flashes of her room. It wasn't just that her bed was darker; it was that her bed wasn't in the gaps at all.

It's all a facade. Is that what you're telling me?

She'd prayed before—mostly for stuff and things to happen—but she'd never asked the universe a question outright. She froze... listening, watching, trying to catch anything that might be the universe's response.

But the overhead light didn't squeal and burn out. There was no lightning strike outside, no dog suddenly barking in the distance. She noticed nothing change except the flickers fading, taking the gaps in the world's film with them.

Karen wasn't going to go so far as to say that the material world wasn't real, because it seemed real enough to her, for what it was, anyway. It was real in the way that video games were real video games.

Although, bleh, she still did not like that comparison.

But to whatever extent the material world was real, it definitely wasn't everything. It wasn't even the most important thing.

So what is?

———

Karen had put her kids to bed the night before with no sign of things to come, but that morning they woke up as her own little personal distractions.

"Can I get a Whatszzyt?" Lila asked as she poured her own cereal.

"A what?"

"A Whatszzyt. It's this little animal you clip on your backpack. Eloise has the lion-llama. She wanted the owl-squirrel. I like the elephant-mouse."

"What do you mean she wanted the owl? Why does she have the lion?"

"Lion-llama. They're in a blind box, Mom. You don't know what you're gonna get. Can I get one?"

"You have an allowance, I guess. If that's what you want to spend it on."

"I don't have enough."

"How much is it?"

"Forty dollars."

"Forty bucks?! For a keychain?"

Lila shrugged. "Can I?"

Karen sighed, torn between gratitude that she'd made it eight, almost nine years before having to have this conversation, and the burning desire to tell Lila no. No, no, no.

"Maybe for your birthday."

"But that's not until next month!"

Lila flopped in her chair at the table and pushed her cereal around with her spoon.

Karen said nothing. Kyle was watching Lila while he munched away on his cereal, and Karen found herself watching him, wondering if he would reach this stage sooner now.

———

Big, fat yes, on that one.

Not long after she'd returned home from dropping Lila and Kyle off at school, Karen got a call from the principal.

"It's about Kyle," she said. "Are you available to come in?"

When Karen arrived, a cheerful young woman in a pink cardigan and a perky ponytail escorted her back to the office of Principal Sand. Kyle was sitting in a chair outside the woman's door, his little legs dangling.

"I've got it from here," Karen said to her escort.

"Oh, no problem. I'll just rap on the door for you." The perky woman smiled at Kyle as she tap-tap-tapped on the principal's open door. "Mrs. Baker's here, about Kyle."

The perky woman grinned at Kyle again as she walked away.

Principal Sand was a woman in her late forties who wore her dark hair in an asymmetrical bob, and she looked tiny behind her huge desk. She flashed Karen the same school-board branded smile and gestured for Karen to take a seat.

"We'll just be a minute," Karen told her, and she reached into the principal's office and shut the door, giving her and Kyle some privacy.

The perky escort looked back at her askance, but Karen just stared her down until she returned to her desk. Finally, she did so.

Karen squatted down in front of Kyle.

"You okay?"

Looking down at his lap, Kyle nodded.

"Do you know why we're here?"

Kyle nodded.

"Why? Tell me."

"Mrs. Lethune told me not to say 'glitch,' and I did."

"'Glitch'?"

He nodded. Apparently, Kyle was obsessed with glitches. So much so that on Monday he'd told his friends at school about his mom's broken mug having two handle pieces, and on Tuesday he'd told his friends about a guy jumping out in front of his mom's car and then vanishing into thin air.

He'd told his friends that the world was alive and speaking.

His teacher caught wind of this, and she'd not only told Kyle to stop telling lies, but she'd also banned the word *glitch* from class.

"But I said it in line after recess."

"In line, huh?"

He nodded.

"Anything else I should know about?"

He shook his head.

"You sure?"

Kyle nodded.

"Okay," Karen said on a sigh as she stood.

Outside the window to her right, a straggler monarch butterfly fluttered around the limb tags of a recently planted tree. Neither looked favored to make it through the winter.

This was Karen's first time ever being in the principal's office. Ever. For any reason.

She rapped on the door.

"Come in, Mrs. Baker. Bring Kyle."

Karen looked down at him and said, "You wait here, okay?"

Kyle nodded.

"No, he should come too," said Principal Sand.

Karen shut the door, leaving Kyle out on his chair. "No. He's fine where he is."

Karen sat in the right of the two chairs in front of the

principal's desk. And she smiled, giving as good as she'd received.

Principal Sand's smile faltered. She said, "Mrs. Lethune has had to ban the students from using a word Kyle introduced them all to on Monday."

"Banned, huh? At recess, too? Isn't that a little extreme?"

"It's become a significant distraction."

"You mean 'substantial disruption'?"

"Beg pardon?"

"The test for whether or not you can curb my son's freedom of speech is whether it causes a material and substantial disruption."

The principal stared at her, confusion coloring her expression.

Karen wagged a finger at the front of her own shirt. "Don't be fooled by the kick-around clothes I was wearing when you called me down here. I'm actually trained as an attorney. So is Paul."

"Nobody's trying—"

"Are you sure? Recess? He can't say what he wants at recess? And it's only been two days since he even learned the word 'glitch.' Isolated incidents don't count as a substantial disruption."

"Well, we anticipate—"

"Well, don't, Principal Sands." Karen stood up. "You tell Mrs. Lethune not to worry. Kyle won't be enlightening her class with any more of his *significantly distracting* topics. I'll be taking him home now. He'll be back in the morning, ready to sit like the silent statue you all clearly expect five-year-olds to be."

Karen opened the door and swept out of the room.

"Come on, Kyle," she said, taking Kyle's hand and leaving Principal Sands staring after them.

Or at least, that's how Karen restyled the encounter as she drove Kyle home, playing it over and over in her mind.

The real encounter had gone something more like this:

"Come in, Mrs. Baker. Bring Kyle."

Karen bent down and hustled Kyle off the chair and into the principal's office. She'd never been in trouble before. She didn't like the feeling of being in trouble. It heightened her senses but shut down her tongue. Her heart pounded in her chest.

She got Kyle seated in one of the chairs and then sat down herself.

"Thank you for coming in. I wanted to talk to you about Kyle telling the other students about something he calls 'glitches.' He needs to stop. It's not an offensive word, but it is causing a significant distraction. The students are asking him about glitches when they should be learning. He was given a verbal warning, and then detention over recess, but he said it again at break this morning. The next step is suspension."

Karen looked down at Kyle, then nudged him to look up at her.

"Hear that?" she asked him.

He nodded.

"Are you going to say 'glitch' again?"

He looked down and shook his head. Karen worried he might never say anything again.

Karen looked back at the principal. "He won't say it again."

"Very good."

"Anything else?"

"No. Thank you for coming in."

"Of course. Have a good rest of your day."

———

"And I just sat there," she told Paul later, dental floss in hand, after the kids were in bed. "I just sat there all yes, ma'am, yes, ma'am, anything you say, ma'am. It didn't even sound like a legit censoring. So what if he talks about glitches with his friends? And what are they really learning, really? It's kindergarten. Learning to sit and obey, that's what. That's all. And here's the result."

She threw up her hands, meaning herself, meaning the way she had just sat and obeyed.

But what choice had she had? Suspension? She didn't know how to teach Kyle twelve years of school. And, honestly, she didn't want to teach him. What a chore that would be. And a suspension would be on his record. The detention probably already was. She knew the climbing-up-the-slide incident was. Already branded a bad kid when he was the sweetest and most curious kid in the world.

Or at least he had been, until today.

"He's five!" she said, whisper-yelling. "He's friggin' five years old, and he told them the world is alive and speaking. I didn't tell him that. Did you tell him that?"

Paul shook his head. "You need a hug?"

"Yeah." She crawled across the bed and flopped onto his chest. "Aren't you mad?"

"I don't like that he hasn't said anything but one-word responses all night, but I get that the kids aren't in school to listen to Kyle. They're there to listen to Mrs. Lethune."

"Well, maybe they shouldn't be," Karen said. "Maybe we should all be listening to Kyle."

Chapter 19

The distractions didn't let up. The next morning, Karen got an early phone call from Martin Tyler's hiring partner. It came so early that Karen had still been in bed. She threw back the covers and pushed past Paul, racing down the stairs to where she'd left her phone on the counter, in order to answer it before it woke the kids.

"We were expecting to hear back from you yesterday," the partner said, a man who sounded like he'd had a lot of coffee already. Apparently he'd called Karen the day before, while she was at the principal's office. "Can you make it here by nine?"

Karen said she could.

But she'd have to hurry.

"You got the job," Paul told her as she hopped into the shower.

"You think?"

"Yup. You're going in for the offer letter. You need me to do anything before I go?"

"Yeah. Just get them up, and tell Lila to pour them both some cereal. I'll be out in a minute."

Karen wondered if the partners would notice if she wore the same gray suit she'd worn to the interview, and then she decided she didn't care. It was a suit, and it was still hanging right where she'd left it in preparation to, one of these days, take it to the dry cleaner so that it could be stored indefinitely again.

She wore the same white button-up, too.

All dressed and ready to go, even if her hair was still damp, she got the kids into their coats, their homework into their backpacks, and their bodies into the car.

Deep breath, Karen. Precious cargo, and all that.

When she got to the school, instead of dropping the kids off at the corner, she parked on a side street and walked up with them. Well, walked up with Kyle. Lila ran ahead, which was just as well. Karen wanted some privacy with Kyle.

She knelt down in front of him at the corner, her suit slacks tightening around her knees.

"Hey," she said, not sure what to say from there. "Sometimes, especially when we're younger, we have to do things we don't want to do. I don't know why that is. But can you promise me you won't say—"

"I said I wouldn't."

"You did," she said, pulling him in for a hug. "You did. And I believe you. But I'm not asking you to never say it. Okay? If you want to have your friends over and talk all about it, or if you want to talk to me about it, we can do that. Okay? It's just here at school that you should keep it to yourself. Okay?"

Don't stop talking just because your words outshined another's, especially not then, she wanted to say.

But she didn't.

She'd read up a little on the 'substantial disruption' issue, and she'd found that some teachers were able to incorporate any given distraction into their teachings, usually making it a part of how they called the students to attention at the start of class and after breaks. But those teachers were the exception, not the rule. Most teachers just banned any distracting words outright.

But of course they did. They'd come up in the same creativity-busting environment they were enforcing. It was all they knew.

The elevator doors opened onto the law firm's main floor, where three of the partners Karen had interviewed with were waiting to greet her: a man and two women. All three of them eyed Karen's second-wear suit.

The man she'd talked to on the phone, a fit guy who was balding and making it work with the all-over-five-o'clock-shadow look, asked her if she wanted anything. "Tea, coffee, cola, water?" He then sent an underling to fetch her request.

The trio took Karen into the large glass conference room opposite the elevator. It looked out over the river a few blocks away.

The conference room had a blond-wood table and high-back leather chairs. A slim stack of papers sat on the end of the table closest to the door. The man took that seat, and the women took the two seats to his left, putting their backs to the river. Karen sat across from them.

They chit-chatted about the weather until the underling came back with a bottle of water and then slipped out the door again.

"Well, Karen," the man said, like he was surprised to be saying anything to her at all, "we'd like to offer you a position with Martin, Tyler, and Gray."

"Congratulations," said the women. In the same tone and at the same time. Karen eyed them. One blond, one brunette, both sitting there with the same tight ponytail and the same tight smile, their legs probably crossed under the table in the same tight way. They were like automatons.

Or non-player characters.

Karen winced at the computer-simulation metaphor making sense again, but she couldn't argue with it. They—like she—seemed to be only going through the motions they were expected to perform, like they were just here to fill out this meeting, to fill out this world.

"I know it's late notice," the man was saying. "But we'll need all hands on deck first thing tomorrow. Our first client meeting is at one, and then we're expecting a moving van full of document production on Saturday."

"Wear your comfy clothes," one of the women said.

"Yes," said the man. "We don't have an office for you just yet, but there's empty office space downstairs that we're working to lease, and we expect to have daycare service on the same floor by Monday. It'll be open almost twenty-four hours, four a.m. to one a.m., so no worries there."

Karen rubbed at the bridge of her nose in order to prevent a frown from forming on her face.

"Oh," the man said, "and we're working with the school district to create a bus stop here in front of the building. A lot of associates have been complaining about the time wasted picking up their kids. The bus depot is just six blocks that way"—he pointed away from the river—"so no matter what school your kids go to, it shouldn't be a problem. They can just hang out on the bus until the bus returns home for the night.

We expect that to be squared away by next week as well. In the meantime, we've hired a shuttle for anyone who needs help with pick-up between now and then. What else?"

The two women shook their heads. Then one said, "Meals?"

"We order in, but that's always been the case. Breakfast, lunch, dinner, late-night coffee runs, whatever you need. We like to limit distractions."

The women nodded their agreement.

"Anyway, we just have the standard paperwork for you to fill out." He slid the pile down the table toward Karen.

But she could only stare at him.

"Oh," he said. "Did you have questions?"

She had a few, but she knew she'd only get a straight answer to one. "Can I think about it?"

"Oh. Um. Well." He looked at the other two. One of them said, "Do you need to?"

"It's just that I wasn't expecting to get an offer."

The three attorneys laughed at that, which answered a couple of Karen's other questions: They weren't hiring her for the partner track. They were only hiring her—and probably only temporarily at that—because they'd hooked a whale of a client with a huge case and it was easier and faster to hire all of the people they'd interviewed for the associate position than it was to put a call out for paralegals. And since the client was paying for it either way, what did the firm care whether attorneys or paralegals did the document review?

"So, can I think about it?" Karen asked again.

"Sure, take the rest of the day," the man said magnanimously.

"Great, thanks. And thank you for the offer. I really appreciate it." Karen stood and picked up her pile of forms. She shook everyone's hands and then escaped to the elevator.

Down in the parking garage, Karen turned on her SUV's dome light and rifled through the forms.

Her suspicions were correct. She'd be making more than Paul, sure, but not much more. Not nearly what an associate at a firm like Martin Tyler should be making. Especially since they were still requiring two thousand billable hours a year, tallied monthly. No wonder they were putting in a daycare. Two thousand billable hours sounds like you would work forty hours a week and get two weeks vacation, but in reality, she'd be working a minimum of twenty-six hundred total hours in order to get two thousand billable ones. That was an average of fifty hours a week with no vacations, and it didn't factor in the time to commute or to make sure her suit was fresh.

If she wanted to see her kids, she'd have to peek through the daycare window on the way to and from the bathroom.

And forget about ever seeing Paul.

She put her hand on her chest and closed her eyes. The clenched-fist feeling behind her sternum intensified.

Did that mean she should take the job or not take the job?

She pulled out her phone and texted Paul.

> Are you busy, or can I stop by?

She hit send and waited for the message's status to change from *delivered* to *read*. Seconds later she got a reply.

> Coffee stand. Ten minutes?

She sent back a thumbs-up, got out of the car, switched her heels for the sneakers in her gym bag, and started walking.

Chapter 20

Paul was grabbing two steaming paper cups from the coffee stand's pick-up counter by the time Karen made it through courthouse security.

"Did you get the job?" he asked, handing her a hot cup.

"Yup."

"I knew it. You deserve it. When do you start?"

"Tomorrow."

"Really?" He led her to a small round table off to the side of the faux white marble stairs that led up to the courtrooms. "Seems fast."

"Yeah, well, I haven't accepted it yet."

"Why not? I thought it was exactly what you wanted."

"They're hiring a daycare service. The guy sold it like it was a perk. Guess what its hours are."

Paul pulled a face. "What are they?"

"Four a.m. to one a.m. I can leave Kyle and Lila with someone else for twenty-one hours a day. Yay. And why would I be doing that?"

"Because you'll be working twenty-one hours a day?"

"Oh, but not just working. Document review."

"I'm sorry," Paul said. "Did they hire a bunch of you?"

"That's my guess. So we'll be competing for that associate position for however long they want to string us all along."

"You'll beat them all."

"I know I'll try. That's the problem." She shook her head and sighed. "I know I need to find something, and I know I said this was it, but…"

"So say no. Don't take it."

"I knew you'd say that."

"Do you want me to tell you to take it?"

"I don't know. But it doesn't seem fair to you, me not working."

"What's not fair? This job works for me. And I've got a great wife who takes care of my great kids and who makes me mediocre dinners."

"Hey!"

Paul grinned. "Just kidding. I'm not complaining. I know things are tight. But something else will come along to loosen them up."

"Like what? I've been applying. This is the only interview I've gotten so far. It's like crickets out there. And the perks are great. Free childcare? On top of my salary?"

"You could remodel the bathroom," he said.

"Yeah," she said, not feeling the need so much anymore.

"When do they want an answer?"

"End of day."

"Meaning five o'clock or one in the morning?"

Karen snorted, because it wasn't funny. That sliding definition was precisely the problem.

Paul went back to work, and Karen walked down to the

waterfront, hoping the fresh air would help her to not only solidify her decision to take the job but to feel good about it, too.

The kids wouldn't spend all day in daycare just because they could. Paul would pick them up after work. And the firm's building was conveniently close to the courthouse. She and Paul could meet for lunch occasionally. So that was something.

She made the loop along the river and then headed back up to the parking garage, telling herself the same thing over and over: The kids wouldn't spend all day in daycare. Paul would pick them up after work. She and Paul could meet for lunch.

But that wasn't the real issue, was it? She could feel that scheduling and logistics wasn't the real issue.

She kept thinking about distractions, about the word *distraction*, about its meanings and connotations. She'd heard that word used a lot lately.

The school had called Kyle's excitement a distraction.

The firm had called tending to her kids a distraction.

She, too, had recently become concerned about distractions.

But she had a vastly different definition.

Chapter 21

As the firm's parking garage came into view, Karen felt an urge to talk to John. But while she was thinking about whether or not to call him, an alert pinged on her phone. She was late for lunch with the girls.

Just as well. She didn't want to bug John.

She pulled into the Panera parking lot and got out of the car, not bothering to change her sneakers back into the heels that would have looked better with the suit she was still wearing. Cecily was gonna *love* that.

She shut the door and locked the car with her key fob. It honked back at her.

She passed Cecily's Range Rover on her way inside the restaurant. A guy in his twenties held the door open for her.

The lobby smelled of fresh-baked bread and coffee. She heard the *pssshhh*-ing sound of a barista frothing milk. A clerk stocking the display case dropped a croissant.

The girls were all standing back from the counter, staring up at the menu, even though they ordered the same thing every week.

They turned around at the sound of the door opening.

"There you are," Cecily said. Then she blinked at Karen. "Why are you wearing a suit?"

"What?"

The lobby softened and started tilting, flickering in and out of view. Karen stared at her friends staring back at her amidst the flickers.

Deja vu.

Except it wasn't, was it? She recognized Skyler's Mary Poppins bag and Hannah's sheer paneled leggings, but she didn't recognize anything Cecily was wearing; she never did.

She hadn't experienced this same moment before. She'd only experienced this same pattern before, over and over and over.

"Tennis shoes, Karen? Really?"

Different words, same contempt. Karen shook her head to set the room back to rights.

"Did you have another interview?" Skyler asked.

"No, I got the offer from Martin Tyler."

"You did?" Cecily sounded far more disbelieving than impressed.

"Yup. They want me to start tomorrow."

The scowl on Cecily's face deepened—

Like I'm a glitch she's unwilling to believe.

—and she quickly eyed Karen up and down before stepping up to the counter to order.

Hannah flashed Karen an unreadable smile, and Skyler squeezed her hand and whispered, "Good job."

Why am I here? Karen thought. Her SUV was just outside; Karen could see it from where she stood. She could just turn around and leave if she really wanted to. But she felt her feet moving her forward to fall in line behind the girls, and it just seemed easier to go with it.

The guy who took Karen's bagel order had a name tag that said *John*.

Karen thanked him, noting that he was much shorter and younger and softer-faced than the John she knew, the John she still had an urge to talk to. She looked out the window at her SUV as she moved off to the far side of the lobby, where the girls were waiting to pick up their orders.

Cecily had her phone out and was texting. Hannah and Skyler were pointing out and dismissing possible places to sit. Cecily had scheduled this week's lunch on a different day and at an earlier time than normal, and their usual table by the window had been taken by a young woman with a striking blond ponytail.

She looked familiar, and Karen found herself watching her. The girl was eating a salad and flipping through what looked like a college textbook. She had her phone laid out right next to it. It was beeping—Karen could hear it—but the girl only texted back every few times it did.

Then the girl's phone rang.

The girl glanced around, looking embarrassed that it was ringing. She made eye contact with Karen as she answered the phone with a smile. "I'm trying to focus, John. Quit distracting me."

"Karen?"

Karen turned toward the sound of her name.

Skyler handed her a paper-bagged bagel. "I don't think she'll be moving any time soon," Skyler said of the girl at their table.

"No. Did you guys decide where you want to sit?"

Skyler shrugged and looked to Hannah, who looked to Cecily.

Cecily looked up from her phone, looked around the room, and jutted her chin toward a booth in the back corner where there were no windows and the light was dim.

Hannah led the way, and Karen followed, weaving around the tables in the same way Hannah was, only losing a step when a man pushed back from a table and stood.

"Back in a sec," he said to his tablemate. "I gotta hit the john."

Karen startled and stared after him, and almost followed him to the bathroom, but Skyler grabbed the sleeve of her suit jacket and steered her the right way.

Karen walked in the direction she was expected to go, but she kept her eyes on the man headed to the john.

Why had he called it that? Nobody calls it that.

Skyler let go of her when they reached the table and scooted into the booth. Karen should have scooted in after her, but she was staring at the empty hallway that led to the restrooms, the johns.

Cecily scooted into Hannah's side of the booth, saying, "Earth to Karen. You're awfully distracted today."

Karen looked back at the girls seated in the booth. They stared up at her, expecting her to sit with them and pick at her bagel and gossip about friends and act normal.

Karen put her hand to her chest. The space behind her sternum felt like a clenched fist.

But it always felt like that.

She closed her eyes, trying to get a better read. But she didn't know what she was reading.

She just knew that she wanted to go. Had long wanted to go. And the desire had finally built up to the point where she wanted to go more than she wanted to stay here.

"I gotta go," she said to her friends as she turned heel and left. The girls called after her, but that just made Karen move faster.

The girl with the striking blond ponytail was walking out ahead of her. She had her textbook clutched to her chest, her phone tucked into the back pocket of her jeans. Her ponytail swayed from side to side.

And Karen gasped. She suddenly remembered where she had seen the girl.

It had been last week, during their last lunch. Karen had been staring out the window, and the girl had been out on the restaurant's sidewalk. She had been standing frozen, like something across the street had so thoroughly caught her attention it had halted her right where she stood.

But Karen now knew that that explanation was merely how her programmed mind had oh-so-dutifully magicked away the strangeness of the moment, how it had glossed over the truth to make it not so strange at all.

Because it had been strange. So inexplicably strange that her mind had lied to her about what she'd been seeing.

And Karen now realized why.

She watched the girl's ponytail sway from side to side. It swayed to the left, and then it swayed to the right, each time rising parallel to the ground—where, last week, it had remained, stuck, while the girl had stood frozen, and not even gravity had been able to pull it back down.

Another glitch.

Karen hurried past the girl and ran to her own car, pulling out her phone to call John. It rang and rang, but Karen barely heard it, let alone registered what it might mean that he wasn't answering. She'd only called him because it was the thing she was supposed to do before doing the thing she wanted to do, the thing she had to do.

She snorted at herself, at the way she was still acting out the programming, at how even now she couldn't stop herself.

But how could she expect to? If the forces protecting the boundary were even stronger than gravity, how could she expect herself to defy them?

She backed her SUV out of its spot and roared out of the parking lot, wondering if following this urge, too, was just her playing out more programming.

Chapter 22

Karen sped up Bullworth Drive, taking the curves at the same speed as the locals but with much less finesse. The SUV rocked on its chassis in a way she would have hated had she been a passenger looking out the window at those drop-offs. But she couldn't make herself go slower.

She pressed the pedal, going faster until the paved road yielded to the potholed logging road that signaled she was nearing its end. She flipped on her brights and looked for the stump Molly had mentioned. The light coming through the trees offered little help in spotting it. Dark clouds had covered the sun all morning and had been threatening rain when she'd left town.

She bounced over the potholes, holding tight to the wheel.

And then she saw the stump.

"Yes!"

She slowed down just enough to find the narrow dirt road off to the left in time to make the turn, then sped back up again.

She soon reached the driveway's dead end, but the vehicle parked in front of the giant cedar tree was not John's green, canopied truck.

It was a red truck with a black canopy and yellow racing stripes.

Karen threw the SUV into park and hopped out, leaving the door open. She peeked around the red truck to see if John's truck was parked in front of it.

It was not.

Karen saw a man walking toward her, around the cedar tree, coming from the direction of John's shack entrance.

Karen halted and stepped back.

The man was too short to be John, too clean-shaven, too young and alert, and too quick on his feet.

And he wore a red-and-black plaid thermal hunting jacket.

Karen's heart pounded.

The man didn't have any weapons that Karen could see, but his hands were covered by black gloves. He clenched them into fists as he met Karen's eye.

Karen didn't know him. Couldn't read him.

"John?" she called out into the forest, hoping maybe he was just behind the big tree.

The man's face flickered.

Glitched.

Karen gasped and ran back to her SUV. Thank goodness she'd left the door open and the car on. She threw it into reverse and slammed on the gas.

The SUV whined as it reared backwards over the dirt road.

Karen wasn't used to driving backwards. But she really wasn't used to men in red-and-black plaid thermal hunting jackets climbing into their own vehicles and backing up after her.

She used the rearview mirror to make her way back to the logging road, going as fast as she could.

But not fast enough.

The truck's red tailgate bumped her grill.

At least, that's what she figured had happened. Her SUV suddenly flew backward out onto the logging road.

She hit the brake. Threw the car into drive.

And she *drove,* flying over potholes with such speed the impact knocked the SUV from side to side.

But she couldn't slow down. She couldn't.

The potholed road shifted to pavement and she picked up speed.

She glanced in the rearview mirror.

The road was clear, but she could only see as far back as the last curve.

She knew the red truck was behind her. She could have sworn it had backed out onto the logging road after her. And there was nowhere else to go except back down the hill. The red truck was there and she knew it.

She drove faster, clipping the turns, praying that no one was coming up the hill.

And to think she'd actually told herself she was following the universe's signs in coming up here to see John. She'd actually thought the universe had been giving her a message using the things around her, the things she knew.

It sounded so stupid now.

Heavy raindrops hit her windshield.

They thudded against her roof and blackened the road. Its wetness glistened in her headlights.

She leaned hard on the wheel, turning left around a curve—and felt the grip of her tires give way. She hit the brake and tried to correct the turn.

But the SUV slid across the white fog line and over the side of the road.

Chapter 23

It felt like her stomach was shifting sideways, trying to stay back on the road.

It felt like her body was floating, yet taking particular notice of every little bump.

It felt like forever was fitting into the few moments it took for the SUV to slide to a stop.

But eventually it did. And Karen sat in the silence, in the driver's seat, staring at the spokes of her steering wheel and getting used to the feeling of proper gravity again. She took deep breaths, trying to calm her heart. She was fine. She was fine.

She was stupid.

She snorted, laughing to make the realization sting less, but it didn't help. What an idiot she was. What had she been thinking, declaring that the universe had been talking to her? What was she on, thinking that *the universe* had wanted her to drive up Bullworth Drive to see John? What a snowflake was she?

And John wasn't even there!

Oh, but look at what had come of it all instead. Look at what following the world's so-called signs had led her to. Who knew what that guy in the jacket and gloves might have done to her if she hadn't gotten away—if he'd even been there at all; the memory of his flickering face made her shudder.

What a nightmare.

But it wasn't real. The flickering effect was probably just the sun. It was probably just the trees breaking up the sun's beam as the light hit the man's face.

Karen looked around for the guy's red truck, for its black canopy and yellow racing stripes, but she still didn't see it. She wondered if she'd ever seen it at all. Maybe she'd made it all up in her imagination, same as she'd made up and attributed a significant meaning to seeing and hearing the name *John* three times in a row.

But it was more likely that the guy worked for the Winehauer Company. Which meant he would have had every reason to drive further *up* Bullworth Drive's logging road and no reason to follow after her.

Karen snorted. Yeah, he was probably just part of the forestry crew.

Rain pounded against her windshield.

In the commotion of sliding off the road, her SUV's windshield wipers had somehow turned off. She flipped them on again, and they squeaked across the window, mostly smearing the rain.

All she saw around her now, through the rain-pebbled windows, was the curve of an empty wet road and the side of a tree-covered hill.

She may be stupid, but she certainly was lucky.

She was only in the ditch.

Had she slid off the other side of the road, who knew how far down her car might have fallen.

The car's engine was off. She turned the key in the ignition, and it started right up.

Thank you.

She couldn't go forward thanks to the hill that had shortened her slide, so she shifted into reverse and tapped the gas. She heard the engine working, but the SUV didn't move.

Bummer.

She took her foot off the gas and pulled out her phone. She dialed Paul, but the call immediately failed. No signal.

"Great," she said to herself, looking around the wet road again and trying to psych herself up to open the door and step out into the rain.

The shine of a pair of headlights glistened on the road.

A vehicle was coming around the bend, up Bullworth Drive.

But not just any vehicle. It was an SUV with a shiny, white-to-pink, color-changing custom chameleon paint job. Karen would have known that Jeep Grand Wagoneer anywhere.

Before she could roll down her window and flag Sophie down, the custom SUV crossed the solid yellow lines and pulled up behind Karen, dipping into the ditch alongside the hill.

Karen turned off the car and opened her door. The ground was further away than she was expecting and she had to slide off her seat to get to it.

She heard the Wagoneer's door open, too.

"Sophie?"

"Karen? That you?"

"Yeah."

"I thought it was you. You okay?"

"I'm fine." Karen stepped up onto the road to survey the damage. "Car's stuck though."

"Yeah. Your back end's off the ground. I can get you out."

"You can?"

Sophie had always been a stylish and put-together person, like Cecily, but a woman in jeans with dirt stains and earned, rather than manufactured, holes came picking her way out of the ditch. Her brown hair was in a high, messy ponytail and she had a big smile on her makeup-free face.

Karen grinned back and stepped down into the ditch, the faster to meet up with Sophie. She hadn't realized until just this moment how much she had missed her.

"I'm coming in for a hug," Karen said.

Sophie laughed. "Okay."

Karen wrapped her arms around the woman and squeezed her tight, then let her go, but she couldn't stop grinning at her.

"You look good. Happy," Sophie said. "Good for you." She popped open the Wagoneer's back hatch. Sophie's daughter, Sara, was leaning over the backseat. She waved. Karen waved back.

"How's Lila?" Sara asked.

"She's good. She says you're not in school."

Sara's gaze cut a glare at her mom.

"No," Sophie said. "She's not."

The back of Sophie's vehicle was filled with sports and recreational equipment. Sophie moved it all around and unearthed a big chain with a hook. She pulled it out of the back of her car, then squatted down to attach it to the back of her vehicle.

Karen crouched down beside her. "You know how to do this?"

Sophie said, "I do now."

———

Sophie hauled Karen's SUV out of the ditch, and then Karen followed Sophie's huge, color-changing, white-to-pink SUV to Sophie's home, which Sophie had said was just a little further up Bullworth Drive.

The whole way there, Karen thought about what she would say when she saw Sophie's mud hut.

Sophie and Greg's property had a paved driveway that meandered through the woods, down the side of the hill. The driveway ended at a clearing that was still in the process of becoming a clearing. Several freshly chainsawed stumps stood on the south side of the property, the side opposite the driveway.

Karen didn't see a house. Just a one-story dirt hill rising before her.

But the dirt hill had a corrugated metal roof.

Karen wilted inside.

She'd been hoping that Cecily and the girls had been wrong, or at least had been exaggerating. But alas, it appeared that they had not been. Sophie really had traded in her four-bath, four-garage home in Golden Hills to live in a mud hut.

Sophie and Sara's doors opened and they got out of the car. Karen got out of hers as well, albeit slowly. By the time she shut her door, Sara had disappeared around the side of the dirt hill, and Sophie was beckoning Karen to hurry up.

"Do you want to come in?" she said. "Use the phone? There's only one carrier with service out here, and it's not any of the main ones. I can make coffee."

Karen looked at the dirt hill—the mud hut. She could feel pity lines forming in her forehead.

Sophie said, "You've been talking to Cecily, haven't you?"

Karen neither confirmed nor denied.

Sophie grabbed her hand. "Come on," she said, and she tugged Karen toward the dirt hill. "There are lots of things I'm still trying to get used to around here, but the house is not one of them. Let me show you."

Chapter 24

Karen let Sophie lead her around the left side of the dirt hill.

And when they arrived on the other side, it was like that scene from *Willie Wonka* when they step out of the gray world and into the colorful chocolate factory.

Sophie had a garden that Paul would have envied, filled with red tomatoes and orange squash, green peppers and zucchini, other vegetables Karen couldn't name, and a smattering of flowers.

But Sophie walked right past it all and turned toward the house.

The front of the mud hut was a wall of windows topped with solar panels tilted at an angle like sunflowers seeking the sun. Karen felt her jaw drop.

"Not what you were expecting?" Sophie asked.

Karen closed her mouth and shook her head.

"Come on," Sophie said.

The entrance to the home was to the side of the windows, under a covered patio with a wind-breaker wall made of some kind of molded material Karen wasn't familiar with. Sophie opened the glass door and Karen stepped inside.

She was welcomed by a cozy heat and a tamed tropical jungle.

She looked around, not knowing what sight to take in first. There weren't just windows to her left, separating her from the outdoors; there were also windows to her right, separating her from the main living space. The floor was concrete, and a custom molded planter box ran the length of the exterior windows.

"Is that a pond?"

"Yup. It's functional. It processes all the gray water and feeds the plants and whatnot. And look." Sophie showed Karen a plant with long, thick green leaves. "We're growing bananas."

"What?" Karen said, peering closer. Her thumb wasn't green, to be sure, but even she knew that bananas couldn't grow in the United States.

And yet, there they were on the plant, a few bunches of little green bananas.

"We've got avocados, too."

"You're kidding?"

"Nope." Sophie showed her a little avocado tree.

"How?"

"It's just the house design. Some genius down in New Mexico dreamed it up. It's called an Earthship. You can ask Greg about it. This room acts as a greenhouse that grows food and keeps the house warm in the winter. It was a chore to build—that's when Cecily was last here; she saw us pounding dirt into old tires—but we're basically completely off-grid now."

"Off-grid. You mean, like, you don't pay utilities?"

"We're hooked up as a backup, but so far we haven't needed it."

"Any of it?"

Sophie shook her head. "Nope." She grinned. "Neat, huh?"

———

After showing her the rest of her home and how it functioned, and how almost every ingredient in the soup that was stewing in her slow cooker had come from the garden or the greenhouse, Sophie made coffee and room at her kitchen table, moving her client files onto the floor.

Karen sat with her, facing the greenhouse and the late-fall sun. The table looked like the same round wooden table Sophie had had in the kitchen nook of her huge old house in Golden Hills.

But her twelve-chair dining set was gone. So was the furniture she'd had in her formal living room.

"Do you miss it?"

"The furniture?"

Karen shrugged. "She space. The city. Everything."

"You know, I thought I would, even though I hated having to maintain it. Although, not as much as I hated paying people to help me maintain it all. But Greg and I made a list of everything we wanted to be able to do, and then we figured out how to make the rooms do double duty and how to optimize the schedule—which is a lot easier now—and mostly, I just spend my spare time reading in the greenhouse."

"I don't blame you. It's beautiful."

"So what were you doing up Bullworth Drive?" Sophie asked.

Karen took a sip of her coffee and studied Sophie over the rim of her cup. Sophie had been closest to Cecily back when she still lived in Golden Hills, and it sounded like they still talked. Karen didn't want anything she might say getting back to Cecily. She could just imagine how their lunches might go if Cecily was given new and disgraceful information about her.

"Your secret's safe with me," Sophie said, reminding Karen of John, of how John could accurately read what she was thinking.

Karen sighed and decided she might as well just say it. "Have you ever heard of glitches?"

"Like, glitches in the matrix?"

"Yeah. You've heard of them?"

"Sure. Had one just yesterday."

"Wait—seriously?"

"Yeah, I had this striped Hang Ten shirt in high school. I loved it. I haven't seen it since high school, but I have a picture of me wearing it in the other room." She pointed off to one of the rooms behind her. "I've always wondered where it went to, and yesterday I was digging around in my costume box—for Halloween—"

"Sure."

"—and I found the shirt in the box. Weird thing is, I started that box in college, not high school, and I dig through it every year. I've never seen that shirt in there before. But it was in there yesterday."

"Really?" Karen said. "That's so weird."

"Yup," Sophie said, like it was no big thing. "Why do you ask?"

Karen shrugged. "It's stupid, but I guess I've been kind of into it lately. Glitches, I mean. Like, thinking that glitches are meaningful."

"They probably are meaningful."

Karen winced. "But?"

"No buts. I mean, *I* don't know what they mean. But if they're happening, they probably mean something."

"There's a guy up Bullworth Drive who's a kind of expert, I guess. I was driving up to see him."

"What did he say?"

"Nothing. He wasn't there. There was another guy there, and he was wearing this red-and-black plaid jacket. I've been seeing that jacket everywhere, and not in a good way."

Sophie nodded. "You know, a lot of people up here have that kind of jacket. The buffalo plaid. I've got one. Greg's got one, too, although the plaid on his is navy blue."

Karen shrank in her chair. "Yeah, it's dumb."

"Not dumb." Sophie reached across the table and grabbed Karen's hand. "I'm not wearing it now, am I? And to be honest with you, I usually am. It's warm in here, but it's cold outside."

"I was at lunch with Cecily, Hannah, and Skyler, and I heard his name, John's name, three times, and I thought... well, I thought that..."

"That you were being told to go see him?"

"And he wasn't even there. Like I said, dumb."

"Maybe you weren't supposed to see him," Sophie said. "Maybe you were supposed to do something else, and the world used what it had at hand to get you to move."

"The world wanted me in the ditch?"

"Maybe. How else could I have pulled you out."

Karen tilted her head, seeing the facts anew. "The universe wanted me to see you?"

"Maybe."

"I didn't need to end up in a ditch for that. I could've just passed you on the road. I would've recognized you. I mean, you do drive a giant rig of cotton candy."

Sophie smiled and snickered, conceding the point. "Yeah, but would you have stopped?"

Karen thought about this, and she imagined herself driving down those wet curves and passing Sophie's custom-painted

Wagoneer—assuming she'd been lucky enough not to hit her, considering the way Karen had been driving.

If she had seen her, Karen would have considered maybe turning around and following after Sophie.

But she knew she wouldn't have actually done so. It would have been too much work on a road that was too dangerous. And anyway, Karen wouldn't have known if Sophie was busy or whether she would have objected to being followed home. Karen knew *she* probably wouldn't like being followed home, even by old friends.

"Probably not," Karen said. "I would have kept going."

"There you go."

Karen nodded, but she still wasn't convinced that the universe was orchestrating things for her benefit. She was happy to see Sophie and Sophie's new home. But she couldn't name anything that was going on here at Sophie's house that was so important Karen had needed to end up in a ditch in order for it to happen.

Chapter 25

Karen and Sophie talked about everything, from Sophie's move and her decision to homeschool Sara to Karen's glitches and her job offer and how if she was spending all her time doing document review, she wouldn't be spending a whole lot of time thinking.

"I wouldn't be poking at the boundary."

"And you want to," Sophie said.

Karen nodded. "I do. Don't you?"

Sophie looked around her greenhouse. Karen did the same.

"You already are," she said.

"I hadn't thought about it like that, but, yeah, I guess I am. Now, anyway," Sophie said with a laugh. "I can't take all the credit for getting us here. It was Greg's idea to do the house like this. I was the first person to call it a 'mud hut,' back when he was first talking about it. But I'm glad he kept at it. I suppose I could have put up more of a fight if I'd really not wanted to do it. But I was scared. It upended everything I knew about how to live."

An alarm on the stove went off, and Sophie got up, saying, "I've gotta add the zucchini to the soup."

Karen looked at the clock and said, "Wait a minute. Is that the time?"

"Yeah—oh," Sophie said, "school pick-up. That is definitely one thing I do not miss. Go," she said, taking Karen's coffee cup and giving her a quick hug. "It was great to see you. We'll do this again soon sometime."

Karen thanked her for everything and headed outside to her SUV.

She marveled at how it would definitely need a bath but had mostly come out of the ditch unscathed. She climbed into the front seat and turned the key in the ignition, and, once again, it started right up. Man, she loved this car.

She turned around on the paved pad behind Sophie's Earthship and headed back up the driveway to the main road.

Karen rode the brake the whole way down the hill. Bullworth Drive was still wet and the turns were still tight, and Sophie wouldn't be coming up the hill to save her if Karen slid off the road again.

The light at the bottom of the hill turned yellow as she approached. She waited for it to turn green only to hit every red light driving back through town to the school. By the time she could see the turnoff into the school's neighborhood, Karen was officially late.

She pulled up to the turn lane's white line to wait for the light to turn green, and a red truck drove past her, through the intersection.

The same red truck?

Karen's body thought so. She was suddenly tense and on high alert.

The truck had a black canopy and yellow racing stripes, and

it had passed right-to-left through the intersection, headed in the same direction Karen wanted to go: toward the school.

She gripped the steering wheel tighter, begging her light to turn green.

Maybe the truck would drive on through the neighborhood. It wasn't like she'd ever seen it before. And it was a distinct truck; she would've noticed if she'd ever seen it at the school before.

But she hadn't. So it was unlikely that it belonged to a parent of a child who attended the school. Therefore, there was no reason for it to stop in the pick-up lane and every reason for it to drive right on through.

The light turned green.

Karen made the left turn into the neighborhood.

She usually took an immediate right and went down a few blocks and then made a left in order to bypass the madhouse at the school and park on her favorite side street. But instead of making the turn, she continued straight down the road that would take her past the front of the school. She had to make sure that the red truck wasn't sticking around.

But almost immediately after passing by her turnoff, the traffic slowed to a crawl. She was in the pick-up lane whether she wanted to be or not.

The red truck must have gone in this direction, but she couldn't see it up ahead. And she should have, if it were here. It would've been stuck in traffic same as she was.

Karen's thumbs tapped impatiently on the steering wheel. It was stupid to have come this way. Karen waited for a gap in the oncoming traffic and then quickly turned into a driveway, backed up, and headed in the opposite direction, back toward the lit intersection. She made her usual turn and drove around the school to her usual parking spot on the side street a couple blocks away from the pick-up corner.

Her usual spot was taken, but she snagged another as an on-time parent, a tut-tutter she recognized, got his son into a car and drove away.

She hopped out and shut the door, aiming her fob at her SUV and pressing the button to lock it as she listened for the confirming honk. She headed for the pick-up corner at a jog, thankful that she was still wearing her sneakers with her suit.

She heard talking and laughing and idling car engines. Pick-up was well underway.

The corner came into view. Karen saw the tut-tutters gathered around the double-slat metal railing, but she didn't see her kids.

But rather than feeling relief that she'd beat them to their pick-up spot, she felt something else brewing inside her.

Dread.

She placed her hand on her chest, trying to feel the sensations behind her sternum. The fist behind it wasn't just clenched; it was banging, like it was trying to break out, to break free—or to get her attention.

She reached the pick-up corner and still didn't see Lila or Kyle. She kept her hand to her chest as she looked around the school grounds.

"You guys haven't seen Lila and Kyle, have you?" she asked the waiting group.

The tut-tutters shook their heads no.

Well, that was something, at least. Something comforting. Something good. Maybe the kids were just held up in school.

Which probably meant they'd gotten in trouble again. Kyle, at any rate. Maybe she should head inside and find out what was up so that she wouldn't have to take a call about it later.

Karen looked around again, hand still held to her chest, and made her way down the sidewalk that ran along the front of the school. Kids and parents walked past her.

She didn't see Kyle. She didn't see Lila.

She reached the front doors and peered inside. A few stragglers were still filing out, but none of them were her kids.

"Can I help you?" asked an aide standing guard at the doors with a black walkie-talkie-style radio.

"Do you know Lila and Kyle Baker?" Karen asked.

The aide made a face that told Karen she didn't. Karen turned away from her and scanned the sidewalk along the front of the building. She heard the aide ask into the radio if anyone had seen a Lila and Kyle Baker. No one answering the page could recall.

"We're checking," said the aide.

Paul and Karen had resisted getting Lila a phone—too young, too early; couldn't they wait a little while longer?—and for the first time ever, Karen was second-guessing that decision.

But Lila and Kyle were supposed to meet at the corner of the school. They knew that. And Karen was supposed to be at the corner of the school, too.

But she wasn't there. She hadn't been there on time, and she still wasn't there now.

She didn't see them on the sidewalk, and she couldn't see anything beyond the sidewalk, not with all the flat-front buses lined up as they were across the front of the school, with nary a gap between them, their doors still open to students.

One bus started its engine, and then the others started rumbling as well. They would begin their parade out of the parking lot soon.

Karen headed back up to the corner.

She passed the last bus and saw Kyle off to her left. He'd climbed into a section of the metal railing a ways down from the pick-up corner. He was seated on the bottom slat and holding on to the top slat, leaning away from it and dangling his head back.

"Kyle!" Karen called.

But he couldn't hear her over the idling buses. Their doors closed, and their brakes released with a loud *ker-pshhh*.

They started moving, slowly tracking their loop around the parking lot.

"Kyle!" Karen said again, walking toward him and looking around for Lila. She still didn't see Lila.

But she saw a red truck with a black canopy.

It turned onto the street that would take it past Kyle and the pick-up corner. Karen looked for yellow racing stripes and didn't see any. But she could just make out the woman sitting high in the driver's seat.

She wore a red-and-black plaid jacket and she had her hair tucked up under a hat. A yellow baseball cap.

Karen's body jolted electric.

"Kyle!" she yelled, reaching and palming the end of the railing to propel her forward into a run.

The red and black truck drove forward, fast, ignoring the twenty-mile-an-hour speed limit.

And a squirrel darted across the road.

The truck swerved to miss it, jumping the curb and coming toward Kyle.

Kyle screamed. Even through all the bus engines and parent-pick-up noise, Karen could pick out her son's voice, his terror.

He let go of the railing and fell backward down the bark-dusted incline.

"Kyle!" Karen reversed course and ran back down the walkway to get around the metal railing.

Kyle missed hitting one of the young trees, and Karen was about to thank God. Except Kyle didn't stop rolling.

He reached the bottom of the hill and rolled over the curb.

The oncoming bus swerved to miss him, and it hit the far curb—*WHUMP-SHCCRRK.*

THUD.

SHHHH.

The bus came to a stop.

And so did time.

The buses were suddenly a bold yellow, the grass a bright green, the bark dust a deep brown.

Karen yelled for her son, but she heard herself draw out his name long and slow.

"K...y...l...e...?"

She palmed the railing that stood between them, that blocked her from him.

She couldn't say how she got on the other side of it—there was still a length of railing to go before she could get around it—but she was suddenly beyond it, racing down the short incline in a straight line to her son.

She raced—she intended to race, and she was moving forward—but her legs felt like they were loping in large limited-gravity strides rather than turning over as fast as they could.

But the loping sensation was just one of many sensory details lurking at the periphery of her heightened awareness. What she focused on was what she could see: the pebbled texture of the pavement her son had rolled over, and how the light sprinkling of gravel had been disturbed; the sharp edge of the bottom of the bus, where the bi-fold door in front of the spent tire was digging into the ground; and the place where her son should be.

But she couldn't see him. She couldn't see Kyle.

And yet she didn't feel panicked. She felt concerned—she could feel it inside her, behind the focus and the determination—but she did not feel like she was helpless to help him.

She reached the bus.

She bent down in front of the flattened tire.

She still couldn't see Kyle, but she knew he was there. She *knew*.

She grabbed what she could of the corner of the bus that was digging into the ground, and she lifted.

Beneath the bus, Kyle looked up at her.

She grabbed him roughly by the back of his coat collar, like a mama bear grabbing her cub by the scruff, and dragged him out to safety.

Chapter 26

With her cub safe and sound, time sped back up again, until it was nothing more than a blur.

And yet Karen still felt high: aware, focused, capable.

Like the bus settling down on the pavement, Karen knelt before her son.

She could see in his face, behind his tears—her high helped her see beyond the tears—that he was fine.

But he was clutching his arm.

Broken, probably.

She'd take it. Oh, yes, she would take it. Over the many alternatives? You bet she would take it.

She scooped him up in her arms and stood.

"Lila!" she yelled, not seeing the girl, just saying her name—and like magic, Lila appeared.

Karen nodded. Good. Her daughter was fine. Her son would be okay. The world was made right again.

And Karen could have relaxed, but she didn't. Her body was still alight with energy.

With laser focus, she carried Kyle back to the part of the sidewalk where she could get around the railing, Lila trailing at her side.

But people stood in her way. People with walkie-talkie-like radios.

They wanted her to sit.

They wanted her to wait for an ambulance.

Karen wanted to persist, to resist, but she was outnumbered, and the sirens were near.

Time continued in a blur, amid everyone's fussing and ordering her around, like they all knew better than she.

And yet in Karen's mind, time might as well have stood still. She was high and no amount of well-intentioned fussing could bring her down.

She saw through it all, through all of the people acting out what they'd been taught to do.

She saw through their facades to their fundamental light, a light that lit up the vast majority of empty space that made up each and every one of their bodies—their lights shined so brightly within them that Karen could tell each one of them apart better than ever before.

And yet she could see how they were also all connected. All one.

School guards, paramedics, cops—shining, they all asked Karen questions, and Karen answered; she could feel herself answering, acting out her part of what they'd all been taught to do.

But instead of just doing it, of only doing it, she witnessed it. She heard her voice speaking, saw her eyes seeing, felt her body feeling. That electric, heightened awareness kept buzzing within her.

She eventually made it to the hospital.

How? She couldn't say. Did she drive? Did she get a ride? Did she take an ambulance? It didn't matter. Those details were all largely interchangeable. She was here and Kyle had a fracture. Nothing a simple cast couldn't set right.

She asked Lila to sit with Kyle while he got his cast. She probably should have sat with Kyle herself—it's what she was supposed to do, what she'd be judged for not doing—but she needed to be in the waiting room.

Paul was on his way.

But more than that, when she was in the waiting room, under its special mix of harsh and dim light, she could see the flickers.

And the way the flickers played with the light that made up the vast majority of every person, of every thing, even the vending machines, was a sight she would probably never see again, and one she never wanted to forget.

The chairs and walls and floor and vending machines were all light, just like the people passing her. But amidst the flickers, she could see that the light of the walls and chairs was refracted light, reflected light. And so was the light that filled out the human bodies.

But in the gap between flickers, where the chairs and vending machines and even the human bodies disappeared, a spark, where the human bodies had been, remained.

"Are you sure you wouldn't rather wait with your son?" an orderly asked her.

The forces want to distract you, John had said. *They don't want you thinking too closely about the world and what's going on in it. And definitely not about what's going on behind it.*

And once distraction doesn't work, the forces will try to overwhelm you, shame you, scare you into not coming any closer to the boundary.

That's fine, Karen thought toward the forces. *But don't you ever use my kids again. Not directly, not even in conversation.*

"Thank you," Karen said to the orderly, forcing a smile and trying to hold on to her thoughts and to her ability to see the flickers. It wasn't the orderly's fault. He was just playing his part, responding to the forces' impulses. It was Karen's job to stay focused despite the distractions.

But the flickers were already fading away.

So was her high. Her focus, her heightened awareness.

It left her slowly, almost imperceptibly. But Karen could feel it leaving her nonetheless. And she was grateful that it hadn't left her as quickly as it had come on. How depressing that would have been. Karen couldn't even fathom the psychological consequences. Good thing the negative forces weren't in control of *that*.

Paul arrived at the hospital.

"Karen," he said, rushing over when he spotted her.

"Kyle's okay," she said, trying to put Paul at ease as quickly and best she could. "Broke his arm, though. It's just a fracture. Few weeks in a cast. Lila's with him."

"How are you?" Paul said, taking the seat beside hers. "The cops at the courthouse told me you lifted a bus."

"Did I?"

"I haven't seen the video yet, but the guys said they've got witnesses who got a couple shots of it. You lifted a bus?"

The moment slowly came back to her. "Kyle was under the bus," she said. As if that explained it all.

Paul stared at her.

"People don't lift buses, Karen. I don't care how much adrenaline is coursing through someone's veins: people don't lift buses."

Paul drove them all home from the hospital.

"What about T-ball?" Kyle said from the back seat. His left forearm was all plastered up, and Karen, Paul, Lila, and the doctor who had wrapped it up for him had already signed it with colorful markers.

"I don't know, buddy," Paul said. "It's been a day."

"Maybe we should go," Karen said, "so everyone can see he's fine. We don't have to stay."

So that's what they did.

Paul pulled up alongside the practice field, and they all hopped out of the car. Kyle and Lila ran ahead to show off Kyle's cast. Paul trailed after them.

But Karen veered off to the left, to where Molly had set up her camp chair. Molly was already out of her seat and coming toward Karen.

"Holy shit, Karen, you're famous," Molly said.

"What do you mean?"

"Have you checked your email? John sent us a video."

"He's okay?"

"Yeah, why?"

Karen told Molly about going to John's house and seeing someone else there who wasn't John. "He was wearing a red-and-black plaid—"

"Like the one—"

"Yeah. And he had this distinct truck. Red with a black canopy and yellow racing stripes. I got scared and drove away and ended up in a ditch. A friend happened by and got me out, but I was late getting to the school."

"I wondered where you were."

Karen told Molly about how Lila and Kyle hadn't been at the corner, about how she'd looked for them. About how she'd eventually seen Kyle sitting on the railing. "And then I saw that truck."

"Same truck?"

"No, no racing stripes. But the woman driving it was wearing red-and-black plaid and a yellow hat."

"You're kidding."

Karen shook her head. She told Molly about the squirrel, about how the truck had swerved toward Kyle, about how Kyle had fallen.

"Well, that explains how he got under the bus, I guess," Molly said. "But it doesn't explain how you lifted it."

"Did I?"

Molly pulled out her phone, made some finger motions, and then held the phone screen up for Karen to see.

The video was shot from the street, from behind the metal railing.

The image focused through the young, bare trees and down the incline to the paved loop that circled the school's parking lot. A flat-front bus was kneeling on a struggling tire, and its front edge, all the way to the middle of its bi-fold doors, was digging into the ground.

Then, from the left side of the video's frame, Karen herself walked into the picture.

Without any hesitation, she knelt beside the bus and lifted it off the ground, high enough that the tire was no longer touching the pavement and Kyle could be seen in the shadows beneath. Karen grabbed him, pulled him out, and the bus dropped down again as Karen knelt in front of Kyle.

Watching it, Karen could feel her eyebrows rise into her hairline. She glanced up at Molly.

Molly looked at her phone again, did some finger motions, and then held it back up again for Karen to see.

Molly had expanded the screen so that it showed a close-up of the video's title: *Superhuman Glitch - Woman Lifts Bus.*

"John has an alert set up to let him know whenever anyone posts evidence of glitches," Molly said. "You wanted to know how to cause a glitch? Well, now you are one."

Chapter 27

Karen's recorded moment may have been a glitch to some, but others were already debunking it. They said it was staged, that an off-screen crane lifted the bus, that the bus's hydraulics suddenly activated, that there was a jack underneath, that the air springs were suddenly re-inflated, that it was just the rebound effect.

Karen didn't keep track of any of this. She didn't care. She knew what had happened in that specific moment with Kyle and the bus, and she knew it was the strength of that moment, of experiencing that moment of heightened awareness, that would help her hold on to what she now knew about the world for the rest of her life, no matter what anyone else tried to say about it.

But Paul found it all amusing.

"Ope, here's a new one," he said a few mornings later while he was at the kitchen counter making waffles. He'd glued Karen's broken cup back together the night before, and it was now sitting on the counter next to him. The extra handle piece sat inside, nestled on a little pedestal he'd made out of junk mail. "They're saying a kinetic boost lifted the bus."

"What's that?" Lila asked.

"I have no idea," Paul said with a laugh. He put his phone face down on the counter. It was Sunday, and they were all four in the kitchen. Karen and the kids were preparing the table for breakfast, mostly by moving her boxes of document review onto the floor.

On Monday, this table would become her office.

She had forgotten to call the firm by the end of the day to let them know whether or not she'd be taking the job, and they had called her the following morning.

"Sorry I didn't call back. My son was in an accident. He's fine," she'd told them, quickly explaining what had happened to him. "But the offer slipped my mind."

Just twenty-four hours earlier, she might have stopped there. But a lot had happened in those twenty-four hours, and as she spoke, the memory of coffee at Sophie's box-covered table came to mind. So, Karen continued:

"You're calling, though, so you must still want me to work for you. I will. But part-time. And I want to work from home."

Maybe it was the shock and sympathy of what had happened to Kyle that had softened the firm's stance on telecommuting, or maybe they were just that desperate for help with all the documents. Or maybe it was the universe rewarding her for holding fast to the other side of the boundary. Whatever the official and unofficial reasons, the law firm said yes.

Paul set the waffles , and they all grabbed a seat. The sweet bread, butter, and syrup smelled wonderful. Before digging in, Karen pulled her hair back. It was still wet from the shower.

She snickered, remembering how, on the morning after the bus incident, she'd found the tub spout leaking. She and Paul had tried to gently turn the valve handle to make sure the lever inside, or however it worked, closed the water off tight, but it kept leaking. The plumber they'd had over to look at it yesterday had told them that a functional piece inside the handle valve had worn out.

"So... not a glitch, then?" Paul had asked Karen after the plumber had left. He'd fixed the valve to give them both immediate hot water *and* immediate high pressure.

"No way," Karen had told him. "Most definitely still a glitch."

Kyle was resting his cast on the table next to his plate of waffles. The plaster was now covered with little drawings and sloppy kindergarten scrawls of the word *glitch*. Next to Lila's plate was a twenty-dollar bill. She'd been carrying it around ever since she'd found it on the sidewalk the day before.

"It's a glitch!" she would say to anyone who asked her about it.

"It's not a glitch," Kyle would tell her.

They had asked Karen to decide what found-money rated as on the glitch spectrum. She couldn't unequivocally say that it counted as a glitch, but she couldn't deny that it felt like the universe was communicating with her kids.

Even if she didn't always love what it was saying.

The four of them were headed to the store after breakfast to get Lila one of those blind-box keychains she wanted. Karen didn't love it, but she reminded herself, frequently, about all the stupid stuff she had wanted and bought and stowed away as a kid.

And she couldn't deny that the universe had given Lila twenty bucks, which, when added to her allowance, gave her just enough money to buy the toy, tax included.

The store that sold the keychains was down by the riverfront, in the section of town where stores lined one side of the street and pop-up vendors lined the river's side of the street. Paul parallel parked right in front of the store.

When they came out again—Lila holding her unopened blind box and grinning from ear to ear—Karen saw someone she recognized across the street.

A man wearing a red-and-black plaid insulated hunting jacket.

"What is it?" Paul asked.

Karen couldn't say. She was frozen stiff. But her gaze laser-pointed at the problem.

The man in the plaid jacket was shopping a novelty hat stall. He grabbed a hat off the rack and slid it onto his head. A yellow mesh trucker's hat.

"Get in the car," Paul said. "Now." He ushered Lila and Kyle into the back seat. "Karen, get in the car."

"Not yet."

She wanted her heightened awareness to turn on, for that feeling of invincibility to take over her. She willed the world to take on saturated hues, for her senses to pick up every detail.

But none of that happened. She was just a human woman in a force-filled world.

She walked slowly but deliberately to the front end of the SUV and stepped up to the edge of the sidewalk, stopping at the gap between her car and the one in front. To her left she heard a car door slam, then, seconds later, another.

"Karen," Paul said.

But Karen kept her eyes on the plaid jacket, the yellow hat. The intense eyes between them stared back at her.

Steeling herself, she stepped off the curb.

Paul came up beside her and wrapped an arm around her front, trying to pull her back to the car.

"Not yet," she said. But instead of gently pushing him away, she held his arm to her chest with both hands, drawing on his strength. She felt the clenched fist behind her sternum open up its closed fingers and grab on to him, too.

She stepped through the gap between the cars.

"Karen," Paul protested.

But Karen stood firm. She was now just beyond the parked cars and almost in the street. She had arrived at where she'd wanted to be, at the distance she'd wanted to be from the person wearing the plaid jacket and the yellow hat. She could see all of him now, including the air around him and the sidewalk at his feet.

Maybe it was all in her imagination, but she thought the foot-wide outline of air around him was flickering.

"I see you," she whispered.

Not for the man. He was interchangeable. He was just the forces' vehicle of the moment.

She said it for the world.

Whispered it just loud enough to feel her breath cross over her lips.

"What?" Paul asked.

"I *see* you," Karen whispered again, just as quietly as before but with more intensity, putting every ounce of feeling she could muster into those three words. She aimed them at the world, represented by the flickers. She hugged Paul's arm as she worked to find her calm, to keep her chest from clenching, her stomach from tightening, her heart from beating double time into her throat. But even with Paul standing next to her, his arms wrapped around her, she felt like just a single solitary spark of light blinking at the forces of the world.

"I see you," she said again, when her body finally started

achieving a feeling of ease, when she thought she had accomplished the feeling of calmness enough. "I see you. And you cannot distract me. You do not scare me. Not anymore."

The words came out calmly, sympathetically, like she was only telling a small child that she could do nothing to mend his broken toy and that he'd have to make do with his many others.

Across the street, the man's intense stare softened, and his brows pinched together. He scratched his head—and seemed to realize he was wearing a hat. He took it off, looked at it. He puzzled at it like he didn't recognize it.

And he probably didn't.

The man set the hat on the nearby hat rack, then looked around like he was getting his bearings. He saw Karen looking at him, and he smiled awkwardly.

Karen smiled back and waved.

He waved back, and then he headed on his way.

Karen heaved in a breath and let it out again. The hues of the world brightened around her—the yellows becoming just a little bolder, the greens just a little brighter, the browns just a little deeper—almost like she was in a dream.

Even though she was the most awake she had ever been.

"What did you do?" Paul asked.

"I'll tell you later," Karen said as she turned back to the car, because maybe later she might have the words to explain it to him. "Let's just go home."

Karen drove.

The left-turn light into her neighborhood was showing a red arrow when she reached it. She pulled up to the white line and rested her foot on the brake.

No traffic was coming. She had an endless berth to turn left, and she didn't see any cops. She didn't even see anyone who could call the cops.

But she didn't turn left against the red.

Paul was in the seat next to her, and her kids were in the car. As much as she wanted to be an example to them of all she now knew and wanted to teach them, she also knew that they wouldn't be allowed to learn it, not at their age, not in this world.

She stared out the side window at a few dandelions still growing in the landscaping, and she chuckled to herself, thinking of what Kyle might do if she turned left on a red.

She couldn't see it helping her prepare him for the world. She saw it only confusing him, only causing him to butt up against it even more.

And she couldn't really say that the action—making *this* left turn against *this* red light—would truly be an aligned act of self-determination. Not with all the doubt she felt thinking about it. Maybe it would be, if she could turn left so smoothly that no one noticed anything off about her doing so. But she knew she wouldn't do it smoothly. She'd slam on the gas, and lean on the wheel, and probably cry out as she tried to make the turn as fast as possible so as not to get caught. It would look like a big, showy example of defiance. Which wasn't the point.

Her own alignment could use some work. She should probably tend to it before trying to nurture someone else's.

And anyway, her kids were already farther along than she was; maybe they could nurture her. They were already poking the boundary. And they already knew that the universe was talking to them. They'd figure out the rest in their own way. Especially if she reminded them that while some of the forces might resist their awareness of the boundary, those forces' efforts to keep them from crossing it could only work against them if they responded with fear.

So don't, she would tell them.

Stay calm.

Stay confident.

Stay curious.

AUTHOR'S NOTE

Thank you for reading! I am thrilled that you picked up this book, and I hope that you enjoyed it. If you want to see more books like it from me, **make sure to leave a review!** Reviews help me in many ways, but especially when I'm wondering what to write next.

Also...

I have a newsletter! I send out updates, exclusive content, and other goodies to subscribers about once a month. The monthly newsletter is free, and you can sign up at meganbledsoe.substack.com. Or you can use the QR Code at the bottom of the page.

Make sure to read the newsletter's welcome email. You'll find your first subscriber goodies in that email.

Talk to you soon!
Megan

MORE BOOKS BY MEGAN BLEDSOE

Glitching the Matrix: *a novel . . .*
The Metanaut: *a supernatural thriller*
Girl, Incorrupted: *a love-horror story*

THE *CORBIN KOHL IN HELL* SERIES
fun low-fantasy mysteries
Corbin Kohl Adrift in Hell
Corbin Kohl Baited in Hell
Corbin Kohl Cornered in Hell

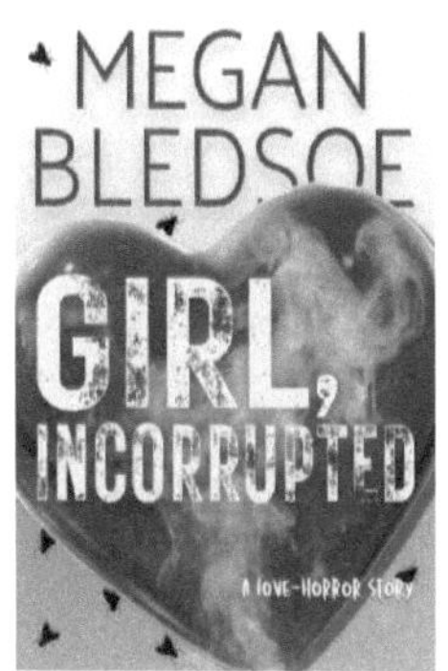

ABOUT THE AUTHOR

Megan Bledsoe takes inspiration from the world's unexplained but still undeniable phenomena. She used to be an attorney but now writes in the Pacific Northwest, where she lives with her family. She is the author of *Glitching the Matrix, The Metanaut, Girl, Incorrupted,* and the *Corbin Kohl In Hell* series. Find her online and join her newsletter at meganbledsoe.com.

www.ingramcontent.com/pod-product-compliance
Lightning Source LLC
Chambersburg PA
CBHW020333310726
48979CB00015B/2347/J